The Foxworth Hunt

The Foxworth Hunt

Dayle Courtney

Illustrated by
John Ham

STANDARD PUBLISHING
Cincinnati, Ohio   2894

Thorne Twins Adventure Books

1. Flight to Terror
2. Escape From Eden
3. The Knife With Eyes
4. The Ivy Plot
5. Operation Doomsday
6. Omen of the Flying Light
7. Three-Ring Inferno
8. Mysterious Strangers
9. The Foxworth Hunt
10. Jaws of Terror
11. The Hidden Cave
12. Tower of Flames

Library of Congress Cataloging in Publication Data

Courtney, Dayle.
  Three-ring inferno.

  (Thorne Twins adventure books; 7)
  Summary: While working at a circus, the Thorne Twins draw upon their Christian values when they and their new friend Neal are threatened by a motorcycle gang.
    [1. Gangs—Fiction. 2. Circus—Fiction. 3. Twins—Fiction. 4. Christian life—Fiction] I. Ham, John, ill. II. Title. III. Series: Courtney, Dayle. Thorne Twins dventure books; 7.
PZ7.C83158Th   [Fic]   82-5561
ISBN 0-87239-551-0   AACR2

Copyright © 1982, The STANDARD PUBLISHING Company, Cincinnati, Ohio.
A division of STANDEX INTERNATIONAL Corporation. Printed in U.S.A.

Contents

1	A Strange Invitation	7
2	Welcoming Committee	23
3	Grand Tour	38
4	Unexpected Guests	51
5	A Greeting From Gordon	67
6	Pursuit	87
7	First Victim	100
8	Sitting Duck	117
9	Visit to the Doctor	126
10	Clue in the Cabin	142
11	Pilot Fish	152
12	Surprises in the Woods	165
13	More Pressures	180
14	Part of the Truth	194
15	The Whole Truth	206

1 • A Strange Invitation

Cynthia thrust her lower lip outward in a perfectly adorable pout. Her black hair caught the hot sun and she struck a bored pose in the grass.

"Are we going or not?" she whined.

Alison Thorne turned to her, suddenly annoyed. "Do you *want* to go?"

Cynthia was lying curvaceously, braced on one elbow, her fist pressed into her cheek. She shifted position with coquettish grace and sat up, running her hands through her hair. Paul Cantrell, strumming a guitar several feet from the girls, was the clear object of Cynthia's coquetry, but he failed to look up. He was sitting cross-legged against a sun-dappled tree.

"I don't know," Cynthia said. "Paul, are you going to the lake with us?"

Paul stopped playing and looked up, annoyed. It was that kind of day, Alison decided. Everybody was annoyed.

"Who else is going?" Paul asked.

"Good grief," Alison said. "Can't three intelligent people

make a simple decision without a quorum?"

"Well, I don't want to drive to the lake if it's only three people," Cynthia complained.

"I don't care either way," Paul said.

"Oh, fine," Alison said. "I feel like I'm in a Chekov play."

Alison had been sitting on her bare legs, and now realized that her thighs had gone numb. She moved to a sitting position, leaning back on her hands, which was just as uncomfortable. Alison was the sunny opposite of Cynthia, lithe and outdoorsy with her healthy brown hair and sunburned skin.

Right now, she didn't feel sunny. Alison went after life like a hound after a fox. Her photography, her music, and her literature kept her too busy to be jaded. Her zest for adventure had literally hung her over cliffs at times, but she woke each morning with an appetite for the new day. At least, it *had* been that way.

Probably the fact that this was finals week at Central High had a lot to do with it. It was a hot June 6th, and finals week brought out the shambling beasts in the nicest people.

"Look," she said, "Chances are we won't find any of the gang. We have the rest of the day off, but they all have finals. Why don't we just *go?* I'm in the mood."

Paul shrugged handsomely. "So let's go."

Cynthia half closed her eyes. "I'm rooted to the spot."

Alison folded her arms. "Then vegetate."

There were times when Alison loved Central High and the park-like area around it. Times when the carefully tended lawns, the glistening hedges, and the quiet brick building brought a lump to her throat. Once she had stood in a quiet arbor for more than an hour, watching the kids pass, wanting this moment of her life to endure forever. Wanting to be sixteen and alive and unharried by responsibility.

A cynicism enveloped the high school today. It cooked in the unrelenting sun, festered in the motionless leaves. Prob-

ably, it was the usual blues at the end of a year. Everything came down to this: all the lectures, the smell of books, the long nights of snow howling outside and the typewriter clacking within, all the pep rallies and homecoming games and candy sales and the school play and the senior banquet—the whole aura of high school boiled down to this hot week of machine-scorable answer sheets and yellow and white lined exam paper.

Alison looked at Paul, and at Cynthia, and struggled to be honest with herself. She was externalizing, and she knew it. Tests were tests, and one passed or failed. She was *afraid,* and she didn't *like* being afraid, and *that* was her problem. Here she was, the granddaughter of the Vice President of the United States, a girl with everything on her side, trembling on the brink—and she was plain scared.

How ironic. She'd faced Soviet spies, UFO's, neo-Nazis, all manner of physical peril that would have driven more delicate young ladies over the brink. She'd survived them all, with her good humor and curiosity intact. But she was becoming a grown woman, and she had to carve out a meaningful life—and that shook her. Everyone watched and waited for Alison Thorne to choose a direction so they could all say, "Well, she's not as good-looking as her brother, but she's sure got brains." Hah! What she *did* have was doubt, and a truckload of trouble because of Martin Young.

She sighed. She *would* have to think of Martin now. Martin, who was running for the U.S. Senate, who was challenging Andy Fallon, the lion of Capitol Hill—and a personal friend of Gramps! Martin, who was *not* a member of Gramps' party, who was an *embarrassment* to Gramps. Martin, the bright political star to whom she'd hitched her wagon.

Yet, the hot news stories were true. Alison Thorne was working for his campaign, because she liked what he said, and because she wanted to get actively involved in government, and in life. And now she doubted herself for *that*, too.

"I'm for the lake," she said a little too snappily.

Cynthia uncoiled and stood. "Not me."

Paul uncrossed his legs and rose like a stork, holding his guitar. "I don't think so, Alison. It's a hassle."

Alison jumped up and brushed off her shorts. "That ends that."

Paul touched her arm. "Let's go get a sandwich or something at the diner."

Alison nodded. "I would like a sandwich or something at the diner."

"I'm going home," Cynthia said. "I have to crack this math or I'm dead."

Alison's eyebrows arched. Was Cynthia actually going to leave her alone with Paul? The girl had to be losing interest.

"See you later." Alison said. Cynthia jogged into the hazy landscape.

Alison walked quietly with Paul, yearning briefly to feel some pang of romance; but the yearning passed. Paul was a good pal, nothing more. She was beginning to think this was true of everyone.

She heard sharp footsteps on the concrete walk and knew somehow they were for her. She turned as petite Jane Cummings pedaled up to her. Jane stood breathless and wide-eyed before her. Paul glanced quickly at Alison.

"Your dad called," Jane managed to say. "He thought you might still be here."

"What's wrong?" Alison asked tersely.

Jane shook her head. "Nothing's wrong. Your uncle Gordon wants you to come to his house."

Alison tasted a strange coldness on her tongue, a coldness that flared in her stomach as well. Uncle Gordon was so divorced from her daily life that she forgot at times her relation to him. She had been honestly jolted.

"When?" she said.

"I don't know. You have to go to Washington."

Alison chewed her lips. "Well, I can't fly there until after my English final tomorrow. I'll have to call Dad back."

Paul had slung his guitar over his shoulder by its leather strap. He looked hawklike, blinking in the sun. "Who's Uncle Gordon?" he asked.

Jane's upper lip was beaded with perspiration. It made her look even more excited than she was. "Gordon Foxworth," Jane said, half in awe, half with hatred. "He owns Foxworth Hall, out on Long Island."

Paul's eyes narrowed. "I've read about him. It's a private hunting preserve, isn't it? For millionaires?"

"I think so," Alison said softly. "I don't see him that much."

"I didn't know he was your uncle," Paul said.

Alison looked at him, then back at Jane. Everything had changed so abruptly. Usually, she could keep her—well, her *connections*—separate from her social life, but not always. Alison could see their eyes withdraw, could see Paul and Jane suddenly back off, as if repelled by something alien about her.

She half smiled at Paul. "I'll meet you at the diner," she said. "I want to call my father back and see what this is about."

"Sure," Paul said.

She watched him walk away. Jane stayed to gape at her for a moment longer, then shot off in another direction. Alison hurried into the school building.

Even though the setting was Dr. Randall Thorne's hotel room just a mile from do vntown Washington D.C., Alison was struck with the terrifying feeling that she'd been captured by enemy spies.

Dad waited in the severely elegant room. Eric was there, too, and they both looked concerned. Dad looked wilted, even in his light summer suit. Eric wore a tee shirt and jeans and was bursting with healthy muscularity and tanned good looks. He had finished his finals two days before Alison, and had gone on ahead. Alison hated him just a little for his big-brother expression. He was her *twin* brother, after all.

Alison drank in the refreshing breeze from an open archway that led out to a small patio. "Hi," she said. "What's all this about Uncle Gordon?"

"I don't know," Dad said. His hands cradled an apple; there was a bowl of fruit on the glass-topped coffee table.

Alison pushed her hair away from her face and looked at Eric. "What are *you* still doing here? I thought you were going to be in that big sailing race in the Caribbean."

"I am," Eric said in a serious tone of voice. "But I wanted to be in on this talk."

Alison's annoyance grew. "Hey, what is this?"

Dad managed a smile. "It's not as deadly as Eric makes it sound. How were your finals?"

"Pretty awful," Alison said. "I think I survived."

"I'm sure you did beautifully. You always do."

Alison eyed the bowl of fresh fruit, and chose a peach. She bit into it, wishing it was cold, but liking the sweet juice as it filled her mouth.

Dad sighed, and said, "Alison, Uncle Gordon wants you to come to Foxworth Hall for ten days. That's how he put it. Ten days, beginning this coming Thursday. He wants you to come alone. I don't understand it."

Alison tasted an odd fear. "Well, he's *your* uncle, Dad. He's only my great-uncle, and I met him twice."

Dad nodded. "Yes. When you were a little girl."

"He seemed okay then. But you hardly talk about him."

Dad smiled ruefully. "Well, we never got along. He was

always a headstrong man, and I take things more easily. Besides, he's been involved in a lot of nasty business ventures and as your grandfather became more involved with the United States government, it didn't seem prudent to—"

"I get it," Alison said helpfully. "Not the kind of relative who would make Gramps look good."

"No," Dad agreed, with a shake of his head. "To say the least."

Eric suddenly said, "Are you going to go?"

Alison was startled by the direct question. She hadn't really decided. "I don't know," she said. "I honestly don't know."

Alison turned as she heard a door open. She drew in her breath as Gramps walked into the room, two Secret Service agents with him. They stayed back as Gramps came forward.

E. Bradford Thorne was a tall, stern looking man with iron-gray hair that was turning white, and a dark, creased face behind steel-rimmed glasses. He'd been a successful lawyer in a successful firm and had made many friends in Washington. He could twist arms and persuade gently, and whispers said that one day he'd run for the top office.

But he was also a devoted and doting grandfather who never lacked for time to take his twin grandkids kite-flying or up in a chopper or skiing.

Right now, he put out his arms for Alison and she kissed him. His light blue suit looked well-pressed, but his strained face showed the burdens of his office. He patted Alison's arm affectionately, and looked at her for a long time.

"How are my twins?" he asked.

"Great," Alison replied, and Eric echoed the sentiment.

Gramps said, "Did you discuss anything with your father?"

Alison nodded. "We just started to talk about it when you came in."

"Make any decision?"

"Not yet."

"I've made a decision. No."

Alison tensed inside. Gramps could be tough.

"Why?" she asked.

"Because I don't know that man well enough to trust his motives. He's always been straight and a keeper of his word, but he chooses to live in mystery, like an imitation Howard Hughes. That's fine, but I didn't want him involving you."

"Gramps, it couldn't be that serious."

Gramps sat stiffly in a chair. "He's asking me not to assign any Secret Service to you. He says he'll provide more than adequate protection, that nobody can get at you."

Alison looked with wonderment at Dad and Eric. Obviously, they'd both heard this already. She looked back at Gramps.

"Why does Uncle Gordon want me?" she asked.

Eric said, "Because he's crazy, that's why!"

Alison looked at Eric. "How do you *know* he's crazy?"

Eric slapped his side. "I knew this would happen. I knew she would find the whole idea exciting."

"Hold it," Alison said, with a tinge of annoyance. "I don't find anything exciting yet, I just find it *puzzling*. Why does he want me there? Why *now?* Do *you* think there's any danger?"

Dad bit into the apple and chewed reflectively. "This sounds so odd that we don't know what to do. Your grandfather and I have both thought and prayed about what to do. As far as we can tell, Uncle Gordon is sane and honorable, and we have no reason to think that he'd hurt you—but to let you go there, without protection—it just seems too reckless."

Gramps said, "We know you can take care of yourself, Alison, but you can understand why we'd be so cautious."

Alison nodded. In her mind, she tried to reconstruct Gordon Foxworth. She knew the story; everybody in the family knew it. Foxworth Hall was built in 1890 by Thomas Foxworth, and went to his son, John, in 1906, when Thomas died. The Foxworth fortune was established in textiles, plus wealth through careful marriage. John continued the tradition by marrying Laura Gentry in 1917. A beautiful society girl, she brought considerable holdings to the Foxworth empire. John and Laura had two children: Gordon and Millicent. Millicent married E. Bradford Thorne, and Dad was born three years later. Dad married Mom when he was a thin young G.I., and the twins were born two years after that. Gramps had used *his* good connections to go into politics, and Dad had fallen in love with science, especially agriculture.

Gordon was a proper son. He was only too happy to inherit the lavish estate of his father, and to manage the family fortune. He was also delighted to marry Adrienne Langley in 1945; she was a wealthy young lady with a rich education and a dark beauty. But something unexpected happened. Gordon fell deeply, obsessively in love with his wife, forgetting that she was supposed to be merely the means to an end. They tried to have children and failed. Finally, in 1947, Adrienne became pregnant, and eight and a half months later, a boy was stillborn. Adrienne barely survived the delivery and was sickly after that, often confined to a wheelchair, a blanket over her knees. She looked pale and brave as she gazed over her land, watching Gordon stride the acreage fiercely, raging against fate. The business tottered. John Foxworth died. Then in 1950, during a dismal winter rain, Adrienne took to bed. She stayed there for three days, while Gordon held her waxen hand. On a bitter, sunny morning, she died.

Brutally strong and handsome at thirty-two, Gordon abandoned Foxworth Hall, leaving no provision for its care. He toured the world, blinded by depression, risking his life on African safari, recklessly climbing mountains, ironically surviving when he secretly wished to die. He enlisted in the Army when the U.S. entered the Korean war conflict. He was nearly declined because of age, but his name made him a valuable symbol of democracy in action and he was accepted. He asked for and got combat duty and wound up in Korean jungles, dying of malaria, captured, held in a North Korean prison camp for a year, released—a walking skeleton, but still alive.

And seemingly purged of his grief. For after the Korean War, Gordon returned to Foxworth Hall, refurbished the house, took up the business, and made it doubly successful. He worked with furious energy, and it soon became clear that his suffering had only changed shape. He never remarried, never saw women. Foxworth Hall became a haven for Gordon, a beautiful prison where he was a willing inmate. Soon, Foxworth Hall became a haven for others: high-powered friends who needed escape from their brutal worlds. Outsiders knew Foxworth Hall as a private hunting lodge, but it was more than that. Tormented executives, lawyers, and other big shots fled to the estate to shoot and fish, to wring out their demons—and to conjure new ones with Gordon and his money. Long Island grew and changed, as suburban developments replaced forests and farms. But Foxworth Hall remained untouched.

Alison knew, suddenly, that she wanted to go. She sensed that she'd find some answers for herself there, and she strongly felt that this mysterious relative wanted her for a special reason. Her senses tingled with the expectation of danger.

She said, "Gramps—Dad—I'd like to see Foxworth Hall and Uncle Gordon. But only if you think it's all right."

Gramps said, "Clearly, Alison, I don't."

Excitedly, Alison said, "But you've *thought* about letting me go. You must have, or you wouldn't have come here to talk to me. You would have just told Uncle Gordon no."

Gramps chuckled. "You're very shrewd, Alison."

A sudden thought stabbed Alison, and caught in her throat. "And *you're* very tricky, aren't you? If I go to Foxworth Hall for ten days, I won't be working with Martin Young."

Eric said, "Oh, Alison!"

Gramps looked stung by her words, and he folded his hands in his lap. "Alison, you know I would never interfere in your political activities."

Alison pressed her lips together. "I'm sorry, Gramps, I don't mean to be fresh. But I know how much it hurts you—"

"Yes, it does hurt me," Gramps said sharply. "It bothers me that the media have played up your involvement with Young, and made me look foolish—" She started to speak, but he held up his hand. "Nonetheless, it *is* your choice. I think you'll learn in time that Andy Fallon is the better man, even though he is not a perfect man. But I can't *order* you to believe that."

"And if I never believe it?" Alison asked gently. "What if I truly think Martin Young should win? And that he's right? Gramps, I love you very much, and I know I'm still a kid, but—oh, I don't want to fight you—"

Gramps stood up, suddenly very tall. "Well, you may *have* to fight me, granddaughter. Because I'm stumping for Andy Fallon, and that puts us on opposite sides of the political fence." Suddenly, he smiled. "But it's not the Civil War, Alison. It doesn't mean that you don't get my special recipe chocolate chip cookies when you come to see me."

Alison felt a warmth inside her throat. "I'd almost give up the campaign for those."

"Well, don't give up yet. Marty Young is a good, tough fighter, and a man of high principle. I could think of worse men to wrestle with in the Senate."

He came to Alison and studied her with a mixture of tenderness and concern. "I can't imagine why in the world I should trust my brother-in-law with my granddaughter. But I know Gordon, and I can't imagine why I shouldn't trust him. If he wants you, he must need you. And if a man as rich and powerful as that needs you, there must be a reason."

"Thanks," Alison said weakly.

Gramps looked at Eric. "You're truly upset, aren't you?"

Eric held back his anger badly; his fists were clenched at his sides. "I think it's—well, it's not my place to say."

"Speak up," Gramps ordered.

"I think it's dumb!" Eric shot back. "Letting her in there for ten days with no protection—he's got a whole forest in there—he's an eccentric old coot—he's—"

Gramps was grinning now. "He's not inviting *you*, is he?"

Eric's mouth clamped shut, and Dad glanced at him with amusement. Gramps chuckled. "Eric, I wish I could shoehorn you in there. But he wants Alison. This is one mission she'll have to do alone."

"Listen," Alison said to Eric. "You saved that girl in Hawaii by yourself—"

"And I nearly got myself killed!"

"Well," Alison said, unable to resist, *"I'll* be more careful!"

Alison felt ladylike and very nervous as she gazed at Martin Young in the hazy light of the Sea Witch restaurant. Not that Alison was awed in Martin's presence; she'd met some pretty important world figures. But Martin, who was twenty-six and very charming and popular, looked at her with piercing eyes whose sternness caught her off guard.

It wasn't just his gaze, though, that unhinged her. This was a beautiful, star-pointed June night, and Alison felt on the edge of something momentous—or deadly.

"I'll miss the campaign for ten days," she said.

Martin smiled at her across the table. He had all the credentials for politics: he was tall and graceful, with boyish good looks, clear, honest eyes, and a mop of auburn hair styled casually, with a forelock that dipped almost to his eyebrows. He dressed smartly, but never radically: dark blazers and soft shirts, muted sweaters and tailored slacks, expensive shoes. Always expensive shoes. It was a vice of his. He admitted to it.

She felt a trifle shabby; she'd worn a ribbed shirt over white jeans, and sandals. After all, the Sea Witch was on the Potomac, and a langorous June breeze flowed through the open windows, along with flies and gauzy water insects. But Martin always looked fine.

"Will you?" he said now.

She'd been drifting. "Will I what?"

"Miss the campaign," he laughed.

She laughed also. "Yes, I will. I've been around politics all my life, sort of, and of course I helped out in Gramps' campaign, but—"

"But this is so much more stimulating than a race for Vice President!"

She arched an eyebrow. "That's not what I was going to say."

"What, then?"

She poked at her crabmeat cocktail for the last shreds. "It was just *cute* that I was stuffing envelopes for my grandfather. But this is—well, involving."

The white-jacketed waiter, bald and unobtrusive, cleared away the dirty dishes. Martin sipped at ice water. "It certainly involves *me*, I'll tell you that."

She leaned forward, twining her feet under the table. "How *is* business, anyway?"

"Suspenseful. We make the big push this summer."

"Good luck."

His eyes glittered. "Well, it's a little more than luck. Andrew Fallon is pretty entrenched. I'm going to have to run like crazy to catch up."

"But Fallon is an old drip. You're young and smart and right and plus your father was—"

His hand cracked against the table so loudly that it aroused other diners. Alison stared. "Don't bring him up," Martin whispered.

Alison felt foolish. "I'm sorry. I didn't mean to put you down."

He calmed himself with a concentrated, obvious effort. He spread his manicured hands on the white tablecloth and regarded them as if they were not his. After a while, he raised his eyes to her. She watched him steadily. A piano played nearby.

"I know you didn't mean anything," he said. "Of all people, you would never be cruel. But so many others have. Marty Young is running on his father's memory. He's cynical and heartless, he's ambitious and mean. I am not mean, Alison. I want to be a Senator. I want to work for my state, for the country, to preserve whatever beauty and bounty is left. But nobody trusts an idealist. There are no more ideals. So Marty Young has to have an angle. He wants to be President. I really just want to make it better for the people who work and live where *I* do."

His voice never rose in pitch, but the intensity was there. Martin could play his larynx like a violin.

"I know, Martin," Alison said. *"Fallon* is the cynic. He appeals to the greedy, to the worst instincts in people."

"Yes, he does. And we're in a greedy and selfish mood in this country. I don't fit. I'm a sixties liberal, but unfortunately this is not the sixties. I'm not tough enough."

"Yes you are, in the right way."

The waiter brought their main courses. The imposed silence lasted as they tasted the food. Her seafood Newburg was hot and delicious. Martin didn't seem to enjoy his lobster tails.

He laughed suddenly, a low, self-deprecating laugh. His eyes sparked. "How can you stand me?" he said.

She felt relieved. "It's not hard."

"Alison, try to understand that it's my life. One thing my father did give me—the love of the game. I'm a politician and I'll never be anything else. I can smell the Senate. And yes, of course I'd like to be President. If a man works for a corporation and has any guts at all, he sets his eyes on the executive suite. But I'm not going to be obsessed about it. I'm trying to do a job."

She said, "I know. And I do believe in you, Martin. I'm defying my grandfather over it."

"I appreciate that," he said. "I really do. It takes a lot of courage, and it makes *me* more honest, I guess."

"I hope so," Alison said. "I'd hate to be made a fool of."

She wanted him to win, and wanted him to prove that he was right about everything, and that she was right for doing this. The feeling was strong and urgent, and made everything around her—the food, the lights, the piano music—more intense.

She knew what she was doing; she was breaking away. Not forever, of course. She would never want to break away from Eric or Dad or Gramps, not when she loved them all so much. But this summer, the summer before the rest of her life, she had to become Alison Thorne, individual, and it meant risking some pain. She hadn't chosen to work for Marty Young on a whim. She'd listened to him in civic auditoriums, on TV, and in print, and she'd done an awful lot of background research on the issues. She'd felt anger at what Fallon supported, and excitement at what Marty said. She'd braved the storm of gossip that attended her appearance at Young headquarters.

But here she was. With this handsome, self-assured, angry young man. Alison, the studious twin. The dull twin. Suddenly in the news, suddenly in demand by Uncle Gordon.

And Gramps thought it was okay for her to go.

Go where? And why?

She prayed for the wisdom to do the right thing, and then she realized that God had already given her the wisdom, and that He expected her to use it.

Their plates empty, they waited. She knew Martin was going to mention her stay at Foxworth Hall. Her eyes must have been too readable. He smiled his cute, crooked smile. "You're waiting for the other shoe to drop."

She nodded.

"Won't happen. Yes, I hate Gordon Foxworth, and I despise the very concept of Foxworth Hall, and if elected, I shall work tirelessly to give such lands back to the public, in whose trust they belong, and all that. But you're a big girl and he's a relative and you have the right to visit him."

She felt oddly angered. "Thank you."

He smiled thinly. "Did you want a fight, Alison?"

"Yes," she said, blushing. "I probably did."

He narrowed his eyes. "Well, you may have one yet."

2 • Welcoming Committee

Alison flew from Washington D.C. to MacArthur Airport on Long Island in an International Agricultural Foundation jet; Dad and Eric came along. The plane landed without incident, and the three disembarked. They stood on the tarmac in an isolated area of the airport. The day was new and just drying out, the early sun yellow. High scudding clouds accentuated a cerulean sky. Alison wore jeans and a lemon-colored shirt; her hair was brushed to a gleam.

"Uncle Gordon is supposed to send a car for me at 8:30," she said.

Dad nodded. "That was the plan."

"It's almost that now."

"He's rumored to be punctual," Dad said.

Alison nodded, smelling the warm metallic odor of jet planes warming up, and the soft dampness of the earth. Long Island summer was wet, the air soaked with humidity borne from the ocean by westerly winds. "I'm nervous," she said. "I don't know what to expect."

Eric grunted. "Trouble. That's what you can expect."

"I have an idea what it might be," Dad said.

She looked at him. "What?"

"It's a hunch, but I'm surprised nobody else thought of it. Gordon Foxworth has no children. He's the last of the line."

"I know."

Dad fixed her with a steady gaze. "I think he's considering you to inherit the estate. You and Eric."

Alison's stomach dropped for an instant, and the coffee she'd drunk on the plane turned bitter on her tongue. "Inherit? That's insane. He hardly knows me. *You're* his nephew. And there are so many other relatives. Gramps, and Uncle Walter's family, and the Langleys and the Gentrys. There's an army of people after that fortune. Why me?"

"He called you. And I suspect he'll call Eric, too, when he's ready."

"Well, for all I know, he's called everybody else. I may be petitioner number four hundred and eight."

Dad checked his watch, as the wind ruffled his hair. "Well, I think it's a possibility."

Eric shielded his eyes. "I see a car," he announced. Indeed, there was a car, pulling away from the terminal area and heading for them in a plume of dust. The sun glinted from the vehicle and made a blinding mirror of it. "I have a better theory."

"Which is?" Alison asked.

Eric's clear blue eyes locked with his sister's. "I think Gramps is really a little worried about Andrew Fallon. I think he wants to know the truth and I think Uncle Gordon *has* the truth."

"Why?" Alison demanded.

Eric said, "Because Fallon was involved with Uncle Gordon in a couple of business deals—"

Dad cut in. "That's conjecture, Eric. A lot of accusations have been made against Andy Fallon. He's a tough old bird;

he's made friends and enemies. He's done well in business, too, and I don't say he's always been a saint. But the rumors about secret deals with Uncle Gordon—"

"They're pretty persistent," Eric said. "Dad, this whole thing sounds like a setup. Uncle Gordon wanting Alison to visit right now—and not *me*—"

"Oh come on," Alison said. "That sounds pretty babyish, brother dear. Because I'm a girl—"

"Because you're a girl who's pretty terrific, but Foxworth Hall is a man's preserve, Alison. It's a *hunting* lodge. I'm pretty handy with a rifle and Uncle Gordon probably knows that. I'm pretty good at tracking and woodcraft and you're not. *Listen* to me, Alison. I'm not putting you down. You've been up against some rough customers and you're as gritty as they come. But Uncle Gordon wouldn't want me out at that place because I might be too good at his game. And you won't."

The air seemed to vibrate warmly with Eric's words. They could hear the throaty roar of the car now. A long black Lincoln limousine pulled up on the tarmac, glinting with the morning sun. The tinted windshield reflected the jet plane, and Alison couldn't see a driver. It was as if the car itself had come for her.

She exhaled. "Gramps wouldn't let me walk into trouble—"

Eric fell silent; he glanced at the Lincoln, then at his sister. With his jaw set, he seized Alison's blue suitcase. She'd stuffed the big 26-inch valise with clothes, more than she'd require. "Okay," he said. "I guess I've got to trust you and Gramps. I hate trusting Uncle Gordon, though."

"Uncle Gordon is an eccentric man," Dad said thoughtfully. "But he's always kept his word. And he's always controlled his own little part of the world."

Alison said, "I hope he doesn't lose control now." She

sighed and attempted a smile. "I'll see you all in ten days."

"Take care," Dad said.

"I will." She kissed Eric, throwing a slim arm around his neck. "I'll be back in time to see you win that race." She grinned at him, her eyes filling.

"Sure," he said. "I just wish I could go into Foxworth Hall with you. And if anything goes wrong, I'll *be* there, whether Uncle Gordon likes it or not."

"You and about fifty trained agents," Dad said. "But I don't think that will happen. Alison—so long."

She kissed her father and hugged him very tightly, feeling his strength and concern. She whispered to him, "I'm afraid, but don't tell anybody."

She turned away, breathing a silent prayer, and followed Eric to the car. Eric opened the back door and wrestled her suitcase onto the seat, then held the door open for her.

"No," she said. "I'd feel like a fool back there. I'll ride in the front."

She opened the front door, slid in, noticing the chauffeur for the first time. He was a thin, youngish man with dark hair, long under the visored cap. He wore a crisp uniform and sunglasses, and looked straight ahead.

Eric leaned on the door. "See you."

She pressed his hand. "Be back soon."

He closed the door. The chauffeur backed the Lincoln up slowly, then pulled out onto the airport road. Alison twisted her head to look back at Dad and Eric and the plane, then settled nervously against the butter-soft leather of the seat. The car was air-conditioned, though Alison would have preferred the morning breeze.

"Hi," she said to the chauffeur.

The chauffeur nodded.

"Are you instructed not to talk?"

"No," he said.

"Well, that's good. I was beginning to feel a little creepy. What's your name?"

"William."

"Can I call you Bill?"

"No."

Alison cleared her throat. "Okay," she sighed. "So much for amity."

William drove fluidly, like a robot. Housing developments rolled by, and trees, as they neared Montauk Highway. "I'm not chatty," he said.

"You're not terribly well-trained either. You should have gotten out of the car and put my suitcase in."

She didn't know why she was being contrary, but something about William's contempt irked her. Uncle Gordon might be a millionaire, but he wasn't going to step on her.

William's jaw twitched, the only sign that he'd heard her. She leaned back and decided not to pursue a relationship.

The drive was a smooth, lulling one. Once on Montauk Highway, they drove against the morning traffic and sped easily through the bleary towns. Sayville, Patchogue, Bellport Station, Haven, Shirley, Moriches, became a sunbleached repetition of shops, movie theaters, dreary streets, and weary people, separated by stretches of woods and great expanses of sky. The sun gained height and the morning shadows dissipated. The day was going to be warm and washed out. Alison became blue as William drove on; a deep loneliness settled over her. Spies must feel like this, she thought, when they went on missions to strange places for unknown reasons.

They were soon past Remsenburg and there were fewer signs of civilization. William slowed the Lincoln and made a smooth right turn from Montauk Highway onto Norwood Road, a narrow, winding thoroughfare that slid through the woods and rambling farmland. Alison could glimpse fine old homes in the June haze. This was estate country.

Idly, she followed roads as William made his turns: Norwood yielded to Lothrup Road with a sweeping left turn, then, after several miles, a right onto Smith Lane, and then a left onto Clutter's Path. This was a jouncing, half-hidden road, and the gleaming Lincoln seemed alien against hanging branches and wildflowers growing at roadside.

Alison nearly missed the gate but she saw it when William stopped and pressed a button on the dashboard. The gate was a massive wrought iron one, sunk into brick pillars. It swung open heavily. William drove through, and suddenly they were in another world. The matted foliage outside the gate ended as if slashed by a celestial scythe. Inside, the neat dirt road wound endlessly through sprawling emerald fields, picturesquely cluttered with graceful trees. She saw beeches and butternuts, sycamores and birches, sugar and hemlock, Japanese maples, Douglas firs. Flowers waved in the wind, like glorious wands of color: tulips, peonies, bearded irises, rhododendrons, roses, sweet peas, larkspurs, cornflowers, marigolds, lilies, and begonias. Acre upon acre of elegant scented gardens rolled by, pouring color and texture against the clouded blue of the sky. This was a breathtaking park, a preserve of the most spectacular loveliness. Alison's heart quickened and she pressed her palm against the armrest, hating Gordon Foxworth as Martin must have hated him, for shutting in this magnificence, for hoarding it selfishly. Martin was right. Foxworth Hall and estates like it had to be seized and given to everybody.

Dense forest loomed at the perimeter of the gardens, and Alison was surprised when the forest fell away and a wide, glittering lake appeared at her right. The lake was expansive, and there was a dock on the far side, with boats anchored. Alison guessed that the lake was stocked with fish.

Now she saw the house straight ahead, three stories of

Georgian architecture on a grassy rise, dominating and slate roofed. Foxworth Hall. Alison sensed a haunted quality to it.

She grew shaky as William stopped before the entrance to the house. She looked expectantly at the taciturn chauffeur.

"You get out here," he said.

She set her mouth. "Thanks."

She pushed open the door and stepped out into a hot, pure summer day. She opened the rear door of the car and wrestled her suitcase to the ground. She hefted the suitcase and struggled up the stone steps to the entrance. As she pressed the doorbell, she turned and noticed she had forgotten to close the car door. She watched as William stormed out of the car, slammed the back door, and slid behind the wheel again. Tire squealed as he pulled away. Alison couldn't help smiling to herself.

The huge oaken door opened. Alison looked into a weathered face, blinking painfully in the sunlight. The man was old, with wispy gray hair that haloed his head like cotton candy.

"Miss Thorne?" the man said, rolling the *r*.

She nodded. "Yes."

"Come in."

She managed an insincere smile and lifted her suitcase again, when it became clear that the old man would not help her. She passed into the entrance foyer and the old man closed the door heavily behind her. She'd half-expected the cobwebbed, dripping stones of Dracula's castle, but she was—happily—wrong. Foxworth Hall was large, of course, but it had been designed and furnished with a genuine coziness. The main foyer, paneled in wood painted a foresty green, was cheerfully filled with stuffed furniture, a great fireplace, tables piled with books, candles in sconces. Massive oak beams outlined the room and lent it a rustic flavor.

The old man paused, turned back to her. "I'm to take ye to your room upstairs."

Alison looked at him. "No. Not until somebody helps me with my suitcase. I can't carry this thing upstairs."

The old man clenched his withered jaw. "There's nobody to help ye. There's just me, and I canna lift bags."

The man continued to blink rapidly, and Alison felt a chill slither up her back. True, the old man was more annoying than threatening, but it was ominous all the same.

"I'm sorry," she said. "I didn't mean *you* necessarily. But *somebody*."

She was aware of movement at the doorway and she heard a voice almost simultaneously. It was an amused, but hearty voice. *"I'm* somebody," the voice said.

She turned, relieved. The man striding into the room was a husky, grinning man with an open face and flame-red hair that curled thickly to his head. Alison was glad to see the man's bulging arms and barrel chest.

The man laughed. "Welcome to Castle Ridiculous. I'm Ed Ginger. Igor here is George Murdoch. Don't let him scare you. He's just an old misanthrope."

Murdoch glared at Ginger. "I'll put ye in charge," he snarled. "If ye like to play servant to smart girls."

Alison began to like Murdoch's gentle Scottish burr, and remembered the stories about a faithful retainer that Uncle Gordon had discovered on a trip to Europe in 1948. She hoped Uncle Gordon would not be angry that she'd insulted such a long-standing employee.

"It's just being polite," Ed Ginger said. "But you wouldn't understand that, George. I'll be glad to take care of her."

Murdoch actually curled his lip, something Alison had rarely seen, and he shuffled sullenly out of the foyer. Ed shook his head. "This isn't really Horror House," he said. "Though you might think it from the help."

Alison smiled. "I admit I was getting nervous. First that nasty chauffeur and now him."

"Ah—William," Ed nodded. "Another prize. But nothing mysterious about him. Gordon's old chauffeur, Morris, died two years ago, and Morris was the last of a breed. Gordon has to hire chauffeurs from agencies now, and the young punks they send never heard of civilized behavior. Some of them can't even drive."

Ed's anger was strong and healthy, and Alison decided she liked him. "What do *you* do here?" she asked. "You don't seem to fit."

Ed lifted the suitcase as if it were a lunchbox. "I'm a bartender by trade," he said, as he led her toward a dark staircase accentuated by heavy oak banisters. He spoke as they climbed the stairs.

"I tended bar in some of the classiest watering holes in New York and Chicago," he said. "But lately I got disgusted with the clientele. Half of my customers were washed-out executives who talked about business like cold-blooded machines and the other half were prancing bohemians, but none of them seemed to have any joy or happiness in them. So when I read the ad in the *Times*, I jumped on a train and rattled out here and got this job. I'm more or less the social director for Gordon. I run the kitchen and the clubroom, make sure that Gordon and his guests get good meals, good service, and good hunting equipment. I keep their guns and rods in shape, have their clothes cleaned and pressed, fetch newspapers and magazines. You could call me head butler or chief cook and bottle washer, it doesn't matter. I meet a lot of high-powered men, and I get paid well."

They were at the landing, and Ed proceeded down the wood-paneled hallway, which was hung with prints and paintings. "I like it," he concluded, stopping at a door.

Alison caught up to him. "You must have quite a staff."

Ed shrugged. "Not enormous. We have a chef, and an assistant chef, a housekeeper, and some dusters and waxers.

Gardeners come in on a regular basis, but they don't live here. Your great-uncle likes solitude, Alison. That's why he locks himself away here. He figures if he has to bump into servants every time he goes for a walk, he's defeated his own purpose. So he keeps the staff small. Only what's needed."

Ed pushed open the door for her. "That's why it's an event, you coming here. We're not sure why."

"Neither am I," Alison said. She paused at the door, had a nervous thought. "What's on the third floor, Ed?"

Ed smiled. "More rooms. Storage. No ghosts or corpses in the closets. No hideous secrets. The only mysteries at Foxworth Hall are stored in Gordon's mind. Why don't you get yourself squared away and then come downstairs for some breakfast? Like hotcakes?"

She nodded.

"Coming up," Ed promised. She watched him retreat down the hall and swing down the stairs. She pushed her suitcase into the room and closed the door behind her. It was a sparse but pretty room. White walls and carpeted floor made a stark background for the dark wood furniture, the pediment bed, and the tangerine-colored Oriental lamps. There was also an elegant game table with carved chess pieces. A hidden message for her? The corner of the bedspread had been turned down and the room recently freshened.

Well, she *had* been expected. Still, she couldn't shake an eerie sensation at these preparations. And Ed Ginger was right, of course. Her arrival was an unusual event. Uncle Gordon clearly had something in mind.

She unpacked swiftly, hanging her slacks, jeans, and dresses away in the roomy closet, piling her other clothing in drawers, setting out her makeup in the private bathroom. She ran a brush through her hair and straightened her clothes before leaving the room and heading downstairs.

Her stomach rumbled, but she decided to step outside for a while before finding the kitchen. It was hard to get enough of the overpowering beauty of this estate. Besides, she had hopes of locating Uncle Gordon himself.

The downstairs of the house was deserted, and she let herself out, breaking into a brisk walk. The day had turned out hot as expected, but fresh and dry. The twitter of birds echoed from the woods and the nearby shade trees. Insects swarmed around the flowers. The quietude was overwhelming. She tried to imagine Uncle Gordon walking these gardens, lost in bitter memories. Or the high-powered men Ed Ginger had mentioned: drained by the intolerable pressures of their existence, fleeing to this abbey to recuperate. She felt a little that way herself. It would be easy to forget her problems here. She wished Eric were with her, but pushed the thought aside.

She realized that she had rounded the side of the house and was walking toward the edge of the forest. The ground sloped upward and the earth turned black and soft at the tree line. The forest was dense and deeply shadowed, with shafts of sunlight filtering down to the molds and mosses at the roots of the trees. Rustlings disturbed the silence as small animals moved about. A flash of sunlit wing described the sudden flight of a bird.

There was a fairly worn path at the edge of the woods and Alison followed it a short way. The forest closed around her almost at once. It was cool and hollow there, and she wrapped her arms across her chest, savoring the rather delicious feeling. She ran her fingertips across the rough bark of a tree. The cold loam of the forest floor oozed between her toes in the open sandals.

Her reverie became deep. So the loud click made her scream.

She covered her mouth with a frightened hand and turned,

heart thudding. She faced the long, gleaming barrel of a rifle, and a tall man aiming the gun at her chest.

"I didn't hear you," she said lamely.

The man advanced several steps. He had gray hair, but a black, thick moustache made his harsh face sinister. He wore a khaki tee shirt and cotton pants and his eyes were absolutely merciless. Alison began to feel frightened.

"Move," the man said.

"I don't understand."

"Do what I say. Move."

He gestured with the rifle. Alison stumbled, turned, and hurried from the woods, emerging into the open sunlight. The man followed her closely.

"Stop right there," he said crisply.

Alison stopped, running her tongue across her upper lip. The man released the safety on the rifle.

"Turn around."

She turned. Her eyes never left the man, or the rifle. She was hot, except for the pit of her stomach, which was ice. The man aimed the rifle toward the woods and squeezed the trigger. He flinched and the rifle cracked. There was a ball of white smoke and an explosion that struck the air, and then a sound that chilled Alison and forced her eyes from the man to the forest. The sound was a savage barking, throaty and murderous, from many dogs. There was a clink of chain and then there were the dogs, four or five of them. Huge German shepherds, black lips curled back to expose their fangs. Snarling and snapping, straining at their bonds.

The man lowered the rifle. "They would have torn out your throat," he said, "three steps further in. Takes about thirty seconds."

Alison found herself shivering uncontrollably. *This* was protection? She kept staring at the dogs.

There were footsteps, light on the grass. Alison turned

slowly, unwilling to take her eyes from the dogs. A man approached her. Very tall, over six feet. Powerfully built, his body straining against the tan shirt and slacks he wore. Silver hair full and unkempt and matched by a platinum moustache. Deeply tanned. Eyes deepset and piercing. His hands were especially notable. They hung at his sides like scoop shovels.

"Thanks, Mallory," the newcomer said. "Murdoch was supposed to tell her about the dogs." The man stood against the sun and it flamed around him. "Hello, Alison," he said. "I'm Uncle Gordon."

3 • *Grand Tour*

Alison looked up at her great-uncle with a sense of relief. "Hi," she said. "I've been looking for you."

"I was washing up," he said. "I overslept this morning. How are you?"

His manner was stiff, uncertain. But that was to be expected. Uncle Gordon did not have much to do with others. Alison ignored the fearsome barking of the dogs behind her, although a shiver rippled across her back.

"Fine," she said. "Thanks to this man."

Uncle Gordon glanced at the man with the rifle, the man he'd called Mallory. "This is Dana Mallory. Dana—my great-niece, Alison Thorne."

Mallory did not respond, but his eyes penetrated Alison, and she perceived a sharp animosity. Uncle Gordon brushed past Alison. She turned and watched him approach the dogs. As he neared them, a dramatic change occurred. The shepherds ceased barking and snarling and began to whimper playfully. They licked Uncle Gordon's huge hands as he swatted them and slapped their flanks. He said something to the dogs, and they retreated into the woods, chains scraping the earth behind them. Uncle Gordon returned to Alison and Mallory.

"Let's go have breakfast," he said.

He strode on ahead and Alison could only follow, foolishly. She was terribly frustrated, and she saw that knowing Uncle Gordon would be a formidable job. Which made this visit a deeper mystery. He did not act like a man about to bequeath his fortune—or a political secret—to a callow girl. Not *this* callow girl, anyway. In the few minutes since she'd met him, he'd been curt and aloof. And Alison was getting sore. It was not her fault that he'd had a miserable life, and she hadn't asked to be invited.

Mallory gripped his rifle devotedly and moved off after Uncle Gordon, without a backward glance at her. He was a terribly strong man, and Alison feared him. She thought that he could snap her in half if he wanted to.

Alison walked dejectedly toward the house, wondering how to leave early and be graceful about it. She'd seen Foxworth Hall. Now she wanted to see her family again. She'd work out the problems back home.

The house was cool and dank after the heat and sunlight, and Alison found herself alone once more. She scanned the various entryways, trying to guess where the kitchen was. She chose a direction and passed under an archway, down several steps into a magnificent sunken room, dominated by a fieldstone fireplace and the stuffed head of a mountain sheep. The room was heftily beamed and stuccoed and featured rugged furniture, woolly rugs on the oak floor, and a dark, gleaming wet bar. Alison caught a movement near the bar and held her breath, then recognized Ed Ginger as he emerged from a doorway.

Ed grinned. "Isn't it a little early for cocktails?"

"I was looking for the kitchen," she said.

Ed held a rag and a can of spray wax. "You don't want the kitchen," he said. "In Foxworth Hall, the kitchen is just for cooking. You eat in the dining room."

"Breakfast?" she said.

"Of course. This is the big time. You took a wrong turn. Go back through the foyer and the second doorway on your right. You'll get the hang of the place eventually."

She let out a long breath. "Maybe. Thanks, Ed."

Ed waved and she turned and followed his directions. Beyond the door Ed had indicated was a hallway, accentuated by alcoves displaying statuary. Alison heard the clink of silverware and followed it to the dining room.

The dining room, to her surprise, was smaller than she would have thought. Four men sat around a pedestal table, on Chippendale chairs upholstered in canary yellow with white flowers. She recognized Uncle Gordon and Dana Mallory, both enjoying pancakes, but she drew a blank on the other two. They were middle-aged men, one angular and nasty-looking, with thinning gray hair and a hooked nose, the other plump and smug, with a ruff of hair around his shirt collar. The men were all dressed casually, all eating in silence.

She stood for a long while, taking in the crystal chandelier, the elegant breakfront, the luxurious draperies and wallpaper, the wood paneling, the red Bakhara rug on the parquet floor. She waited for some acknowledgement. The men continued to eat.

"Excuse me," she said, finally. The men looked up, annoyed.

"What is it?" Uncle Gordon asked.

"I'm here," she said evenly.

Uncle Gordon wiped syrup from the corner of his mouth. "Sit down," he said.

She felt idiotic, and wanted to do something angry and vengeful—something at least to make them acknowledge her presence. She chose an empty chair between Uncle Gordon and the plump man. A place setting had been prepared, and now a sullen boy in a white jacket appeared with a glass of orange juice. He set the orange juice before her and she drank it.

A platter of pancakes stood on the table, along with a silver pitcher of syrup and a coffeepot. There was also a plate of bacon and a plate of toast. Alison quietly asked for these things and they were passed to her without comment. She filled her plate and poured milk into a glass. She began to eat, but the food stuck in her throat.

"Did I offend somebody?" she asked.

Uncle Gordon looked at her. "We're eating."

She returned his look. "But can't you even speak to each other?"

Uncle Gordon seemed pained. "We don't talk much at Foxworth Hall," he said. "My friends come here to get away from words, from the necessity of making small talk. Silence is one of the major attractions of my home."

"Wonderful," she said.

She returned to her breakfast, seething. Uncle Gordon looked guilty, and tapped on the edge of the table. He cleared his throat. "I suppose I should introduce you to everybody. The man on your right is Dr. Jonas Preston. He's the executive director of Westwood General Hospital, the most prestigious private hospital and teaching center on Long Island. Dr. Preston is one of the most powerful medical men in the country."

There was a small note of triumph in Uncle Gordon's voice, as if Alison deserved to be chastised for making trouble. Alison turned her head as Dr. Preston chuckled.

"You can write all of that on my resume," he said in a low voice. "When Caryl Mason is through with me."

He stabbed his pancakes savagely, and Alison saw that he

perspired heavily. Uncle Gordon watched Dr. Preston for a moment, then turned his attention to the other stranger.

"This is Cory Shaw," he said. "Corporate attorney. Has engineered several vital mergers for the biggest conglomerates."

Shaw looked at Uncle Gordon, and the bony man's eyes glittered. "Stop it," he hissed.

Uncle Gordon looked again at Alison. "You already met Dana Mallory. He's a builder—some of the biggest developments on Long Island and in Florida; now he builds luxury condominiums and private homes. Started as stock boy in a lumberyard."

Mallory drew a napkin across his moustache and glanced at Uncle Gordon, but said nothing. Alison caught the glance and she didn't care for it.

"Now you know everybody," Uncle Gordon said, "so eat your breakfast. When you're finished, I'll show you around."

Alison was caught unaware by the promise, and wanted to say something, but Uncle Gordon was back at his food, totally disinterested. She looked around the table, feeling that something was terribly wrong, but not able to put her finger on it. And the more time that went by, the less reason she could imagine for coming here. She was an intruder, not a guest.

Unless she was not seeing something important. She swallowed her milk and decided to keep watching.

Uncle Gordon, it seemed, had a habit of running—or at least striding. Alison doubled her pace to catch up with him as they neared the edge of the forest. She heard that Uncle Gordon was in good condition, but the reality was better than the legend. At sixty-five, he held himself erect and walked quickly, and displayed not a trace of age in his words or movements. His hands did not tremble, though the skin was wrinkled and liver-spotted. The lines in his face produced the effect of cracked leather. Alison could not help feeling a touch awed in his presence.

She stiffened as they entered the woods. She bit her lip and stayed behind Uncle Gordon, as they penetrated further than she had done earlier. The dogs rumbled and now she saw them, lying contentedly, chained to trees. They eyed her as she passed and her legs nearly gave way, but not one of the animals moved. Once past the dogs, Alison relaxed and again soaked up the dark majesty of the woods.

"There are four paths," Uncle Gordon said. "Three of them come out behind the house. One simply extends further into the woods. There's only one way in and out of the estate. The road you took."

She wondered if he meant a warning by that. "How big is the place?" she said.

"Three hundred acres, more or less," Uncle Gordon said. "Grandfather Tom could have had more—up to fourteen hundred, actually—but he couldn't see the reason of it. He just wanted a place to hang his hat."

"Some place," Alison said.

"Well, I would have taken the fourteen hundred. But that belongs to others now. It doesn't matter. I keep these woods well stocked with deer, rabbit, and quail. The lake is full of fish. There's enough recreation."

"And protection," she offered.

Uncle Gordon looked down at her. "There are dogs at the start of every path, as well as at the main gate. They will kill. You must always use this path to explore the woods. The dogs know you, and they've seen you with me. They won't bother you now."

She laughed nervously. "Why not introduce me to the other dogs and give me a choice?"

"No," Uncle Gordon said. "I want to know what path you'll use, at all times."

She stopped, forcing him to stop. "Why?" she asked.

Uncle Gordon's face was an unreadable mask. "You ask a lot of questions."

"Well, that's what they teach us in school, Uncle Gordon. To ask questions. I want to know lots of things. Like why you invited me here, and why you're treating me like a leper."

Uncle Gordon plucked a leaf from a tree and crumpled it in his hand. "I've been alive for a long time," he said slowly. "Sometimes, I can't remember things that happened years ago. How old are you, Alison?"

"Sixteen."

"I was sixteen. I was very strong, very brash. I can remember moments. I see myself on a horse, galloping along a river bank. I see myself swimming in whitewater. Moments, but that's all. Whole portions of my life are gone, buried in my mind. Useless to me. It's like dragging around a great weight. You're a bright and attractive young girl."

A chilly wind ruffled the trees and brushed her face. "Eric is really the attractive one."

He peered at her studiously. "You are beautiful with spirit and intelligence and life. You have a good strong face, a well-exercised and supple body. You look as though you enjoy being yourself."

She nodded. "I like to get out and do things."

"You can swim here," he said. "We have a pool in the house, but I think you'd prefer the lake. It's absolutely pure. Did you bring a bathing suit?"

"Yes."

"Good." He moved on and she walked behind him. They walked in silence for a long time, Alison breathing the odor of the summer earth, the sap and the leaves. They were in a universe of forest now, and she realized she'd be lost without the path.

Alison noticed other paths cutting into theirs. One had appeared not too long after they'd entered the woods. Another had joined further on. A third path materialized on their left.

"Now you've seen all four," Uncle Gordon remarked. "Just before the hunters' cabin, you'll see the other end of the second path that hooked up with ours."

The first scuffle of a rabbit in the underbrush had startled Alison, but now she welcomed the signs of teeming life hidden in the foliage. She wasn't too pleased with the lizards and beetles that crawled across her sandals, but she wasn't afraid of such creatures. She smiled, remembering her tomboy days, when she'd kept frogs in her backyard.

They rounded a curve, and the path promised by Uncle Gordon turned up on schedule. The path plunged deep into the woods and disappeared in the maze of trunks and branches. Now they turned another corner, and the hunters' cabin was before them. It was the size of a small ranch-style home, done in wood, with a low roof. She followed Uncle Gordon to the door.

He opened the cabin door and led her inside. As he flicked on the light, she saw that this was a comfortable, well-appointed bungalow, with beds, chairs, a kitchenette, bathroom, and phone.

"This is a rest stop," Uncle Gordon explained. "Lets a guest spend the whole day in the woods without having to run back to the main house for food or rest. I always keep the larder stocked and the phone connects to the main house in case of emergency."

He let her look around for a moment longer, then turned off the light and closed the door behind her as she emerged. He carefully led her back along the same path they'd used coming, and Alison recalled his dictum never to stray from this path.

Uncle Gordon was not a capricious man. He'd carefully avoided answering her direct questions before. But he was telling her things all the same. He was informing her that she was here for a reason, that he expected something to happen, and he wanted to know where she was when it happened. His tour had deliberately included the hunters' cabin with its phone, and a lesson in the location of all paths. He wanted her to know where danger might emerge and how to escape it.

She shivered as they walked back. Uncle Gordon had promised Gramps that she *wouldn't* be in danger. He'd evidently lied. What else had he lied about?

Alison lay awake that night, wrapped in pure darkness, listening to crickets outside, and the frogs by the lake. She stared at the ceiling. She was tired and pleasantly achy. The lake had been cold and blue and she'd swum for most of the afternoon, deliciously alone and at one with her surroundings. Lunch had been sandwiches served on the back terrace, and dinner was succulent steak and fresh broccoli and Long Island potatoes. The company remained aloof and even hostile, but it didn't hurt as much. A growing stretchiness claimed her, a widening relaxation. She began to understand the healing balm of Foxworth Hall. It worked slowly, flowering out of the initial loneliness and fear. She welcomed it.

But she still had to contend with a teeming brain tonight, and a sharp sense of terror. She thought of Mallory, Preston, and Shaw, asleep in other rooms, with access to rifles, and she thought of Murdoch. And of the killer dogs. She was in enemy territory, and it was a chilling sensation.

A terrific thump on her bedroom door brought Alison out of a deep sleep. She opened her eyes to bright sunlight and stared around the room, her heart trip-hammering.

There was deathly silence, then another thump. Somebody was pounding on the door! Now the doorknob rattled. Alison slipped out of bed, fumbled for a robe in the closet, and pulled the robe on over her nightdress. Tying a hasty knot in the sash, she padded to the door.

"Who is it?" she demanded.

"What?"

The voice was male, and young. She was surprised. Visions of Mallory, or even Uncle Gordon, had flashed through her mind. "Who is it?" she asked again.

"Who are *you?*" the voice returned.

"Oh—" She unlatched the door and pulled it open, coming face-to-face with a confused young man. Alison judged him to be about twenty or so; he was her height, with thick sandy hair, a spray of freckles on his nose, and a puzzled expression. He gripped a flight bag in one hand and a heavy suitcase rested against his leg.

"Hello," he said. "I think I have the wrong room."

"I think so," she agreed. "Who are you?"

"I'm Jeff Harmon," he said. "The old family retainer downstairs told me to go to my room. Third door on my right, he said. This is it."

"George Murdoch," she murmured. "He was wrong, Mr. Harmon."

"Don't call me Mr. Harmon. Not when you and I are the only people here under sixty."

She smiled politely. He was a bit sophomoric, and she was a bit irritated.

"All right. Jeff. George Murdoch gave you the wrong room. And what are you doing here anyway?"

She pulled the collar of her robe more tightly around her throat, aware of a deep chill in the air. Jeff said, "I was invited. What's your alibi?"

Now she smiled genuinely. "I'm sorry. Just yesterday I was nearly in tears because I got the cold shoulder and now I'm brushing *you* off. I'm Alison Thorne. I'm Gordon Foxworth's great-niece and I was also invited."

His eyes widened. "Alison Thorne! Brad Thorne's granddaughter?"

She nodded, feeling foolish and flattered. Usually, Eric got this kind of treatment.

Jeff offered his hand. "Wow. I am *happy* to be here."

She took the hand. "I think I'm happy about you, too. It hasn't exactly been a wild round of parties."

Jeff craned his neck to peer around the corridor. "It does look sort of dismal. But I've got to reserve judgment. I'm here to do a story on this place. Pictures and everything."

Alison raised her eyebrows. She was surprised that Uncle Gordon would allow such a thing.

"For what magazine?" she asked, piqued by her own interest in photography and journalism.

"*The Islander*. Very glossy, very beautiful. Very pretentious. But I'm a journalist and it's pleasant work."

Jimmy Olsen, she couldn't help thinking. But she said, "I'm impressed."

He grinned. "Most people aren't. Anyway, I think I ought to find my room. Then I can get down to important matters, like three or four hours of sleep. Foxworth's zombie honked for me in the middle of a sweet dream."

"William," she said, amused.

"Was that his name? I wasn't sure if he was breathing. I don't know why Foxworth sent a chauffeur to get me, anyway. I have a valid driver's license and only three parking tickets to my name."

Alison frowned. Again, the sense of something ominous, a hidden purpose, stirred, but she couldn't place it.

"You can probably take any room that's empty," she said. "But don't go bashing your suitcase against doors. There are some nasty men staying here."

"I know," Jeff said. "Dr. Jonas Preston, Cory Shaw, and Dana Mallory."

"How did you know that?"

"We've been doing groundwork on Foxworth and his

home. These men are business partners of your Uncle Gordon. Scuttlebutt is that they're putting together a lucrative deal that's not going to be terrific for the heritage and ecology of Long Island."

"Is that so?" Alison said.

"Probably. Of course, we're not big on investigative stuff, so our angle is the trio of high-rolling men who got into deep trouble and came to Foxworth Hall for rest and recreation. Just like Gordon did when life got rough. A nice human touch."

She brushed a hand through her sleep-tangled hair. "I didn't know these men were in trouble."

"Oh, they've got big problems, Alison. The board of Dr. Preston's hospital is pulling a power play to kick him out, Cory Shaw just bungled a billion-dollar merger, and Dana Mallory is in debt to the mob up to his moustache. Could even be that this new deal will give them the clout and capital to beat their other woes. They didn't come here to take pot-shots at rabbits, that's for sure." He shrugged. "Well, I'd better resume my search for a bed. When do they serve breakfast around here?"

"About nine, I think. You can ask Ed Ginger. He's the only civil person on the premises."

"Except for you," Jeff grinned. "You're *very* civil."

He lifted his suitcase and continued down the hall. Alison closed her door and leaned against it. She watched the patterns of sunlight as they sifted through her curtains. Things were starting to make sense. Like the reaction of the three men at the breakfast table yesterday when Uncle Gordon made his glowing introductions. Uncle Gordon had been playing with them, deliberately taunting them. Maybe showing who was boss before he talked terms on whatever rotten deal they were cooking up. There sure was a lot more to Foxworth Hall than the family legends told. This was not a simple playground for the elite. It was a war room for the embattled.

But that didn't explain why *she* was here. There was apparently no explanation for that at all.

At least not one that she would care to consider.

4 • Unexpected Guests

Alison dolphined under the cold water and swam gracefully, her eyes open to the deep blues and violets of the lake. The icy sensation was bracing and she broke the surface, gasping.

She saw Jeff coming from the house and she swam toward shore. Jeff seemed nice enough, though she hadn't had much chance to speak with him yesterday. By the time Ed Ginger had straightened out the mess with rooms, and by the time Jeff had gotten settled, he needed to stay in his room to prepare his story. They'd met at the dinner table, but the dismal trio of Shaw, Preston, and Mallory tended to dim conversation. Alison found herself dog-tired after dinner, and after an hour or so of nodding in the foyer, she stumbled upstairs and fell into a deep sleep.

It had been the sudden burst of exercise, of course, and today she felt super. She stroked harder and reached shallow water as Jeff approached. He was walking backwards, snapping pictures with a Nikon.

"Watch out," she called. "You'll fall in."

Jeff turned and gave her a smile. He held up the camera, then focused on her as her feet found the lake's soft bottom. She stood up, the water reaching her waist, and she struck a pose, hands on hips, head tilted slightly. Jeff snapped two pictures. She waded ashore to meet him.

"I'll take an eight-by-ten and six wallets," she chided.

He laughed. "I have to account for the film. They'll ask me about the shot of you."

"Local fauna," she said. "I didn't realize you were a photographer also."

"It helped me get hired," he said. "*The Islander* is not given to hiring guys just out of college, but taking my own pictures convinced them that I was a bargain. I save them the price of another man on assignments."

"Or woman," she said pointedly. She dried her hands and arms with a towel she'd left on the shore, and Jeff let her examine the camera. Her own Nikon outfit was secondhand, but this was new, and Alison grew excited over the various electronic features.

The sun sparkled on the droplets that clung to her skin. "How long will you be here, Jeff?"

He shrugged. "Two or three days. As long as it takes to get the material. How about you?"

"Ten days," she said. "Uncle Gordon invited me specifically for ten days. I don't understand why."

"Then cut it short," he said. "And I'll take you to a movie. Do Vice Presidents' granddaughters go to movies?"

She smiled. "Sometimes. How come you're not awestruck anymore?"

"I *am*. I'm trying to get over it. Are we on?"

She cast her eyes to the ground, studying the grass. She didn't want to tell him he was just a little too brash and slick for her taste; after all, he *was* a decent guy. "Jeff, when I leave here, I've got to get back to Washington, and get ready to go back to school in the fall—"

"For two months?"

She looked at him and said hastily, "And I've gotten myself involved in some political work that's going to keep me hopping. I don't think I could commute to Long Island and back—"

Jeff tightened his mouth, nodded. "Okay, I'm not dense. Win a few, lose a few."

"I'm sorry."

"Don't be sorry. I wouldn't expect a girl like you to be available."

She smiled gently. "Thank you. I'm not really unavailable; just busy—and I won't be *here* very long."

Jeff checked a setting on the camera before speaking. "Who is he? Is he a brilliant young turk?"

"Who?"

"The politician you're working for."

"Oh," she said. "Well, sort of. Maybe you know of him—he's running for the Senate. Martin Young."

Jeff laughed. "Sure I know *of* him. I wrote a story on him for my high-school newspaper some years back. Up and coming young politicians on the Island. I heard he didn't care for the story."

"Were you nasty?"

"No. Just perceptive. But if you and Young are—working together, I'd rather not go into it."

"Hey," she said sharply. "If *that's* what you're thinking, you'd better—"

The drone of a car caused them to turn their heads. William's Lincoln wound along the path to the house.

"More guests," Jeff said.

"Uncle Gordon seems to be getting up quite a party," Alison mused. "Very strange for a recluse."

Jeff smiled at her. "You're dramatic."

"No, just logical. When a person radically changes his behavior pattern, there's a reason for it."

The Lincoln stopped, and William emerged lethargically. He opened the rear door and two people stepped out, a man and a woman. At this distance, it was hard to see faces. The man wore a light blue suit and seemed to be of average height, with gray hair and a husky frame. The woman was a touch shorter, on the youngish side, in a lemon-colored travelling suit. They looked wilted.

"I didn't think wives were allowed on the preserve," Alison said.

"You don't know if she's his wife."

Alison ignored him. "Preston, Mallory, and Shaw are strictly stag. I gathered that Uncle Gordon ran a man's retreat."

"You're here." Jeff strained to see the couple as they removed suitcases from the car. "You know, he looks familiar, but he couldn't be who I think he is."

Alison looked at Jeff. "Who do you think he is?"

"You wouldn't believe it."

"Sure I would."

Jeff snapped the lens cap onto his camera. "Who were we talking about just now?"

"Jeff, that is *not* Martin Young."

"No, But I think it's Andrew Fallon."

Alison's chest tightened. There was no reason for it, of course. Andrew Fallon was not her *personal* enemy. But still, it was somehow embarrassing to be here with him.

"Let's go see," she said.

"I was on my way."

They jogged the distance between the lake and the house, and Alison was dry by the time they reached the front portico. She wore a light, lace-trimmed beach jacket over her bathing suit. William was sliding into the Lincoln. The new couple had already gone inside. William glared at Alison for a moment, then slammed the car door and drove away.

"He's earning his salary these days," Jeff said.

They mounted the steps and Jeff pushed the front door open. Alison felt embarrassed to be dressed in only her beach garb, although Ed Ginger had assured her that it was all right to parade through the house informally. This feeling didn't help when she and Jeff came upon the couple the moment they were inside.

And there was no doubt who the man was.

Andrew Fallon and his wife stood in the center of the foyer, adrift in a sea of baggage. Alison recognized him at once: the close-cropped hair, the angry, strained face, the bantam's body, cocked for a fight. He stood now with his hands on his hips, his mouth a tight line. Alison had seen Laura Fallon on a couple of her husband's campaign commercials. She was a wispy woman, perspiring genteelly, timid in her husband's shadow. Her hair was well-coiffed, and she looked older than she had from the lake.

Jeff slung his camera over his shoulder as both Fallons turned to look at the newcomers.

"Hello, Mr. Fallon," Alison said.

Fallon's eyes narrowed as he recognized the girl, and then he brightened. "Alison, how are you?"

The Fallon smile—terse, toothy—flashed on, and Fallon patted her shoulder as he pumped her hand eagerly. *Campaigning all the time,* Alison thought.

"I'm okay, Mr. Fallon. What brings you out here?"

"Besides William's limousine," Jeff put in breezily.

Fallon glared at Jeff, then said to Alison, "Rest and recreation. Time off from a hot and nasty campaign. Gordon Foxworth generously invited me here for a day or two to gather my wits. Can't rest at any local hostelry, of course. People recognize me. Media gets all over me."

He glanced nervously at Jeff, not certain if he should be so candid. Alison saw the byplay.

"This is Jeff Harmon, reporter for *The Islander.*"

Fallon's eyes pierced him. "More media. I'm not pleased. Haven't I seen you before?"

"I interviewed you once when I was in high school," Jeff said, positively beaming at being remembered. Alison saw how Fallon made friends.

Laura Fallon, until now mute and retiring, cocked her head to one side, considering Alison. "Drew," she said, in a throaty voice. "Why is she here?"

Fallon glanced at Laura, apparently surprised to find her there. "She's Gordon's great-niece, Dear."

"I know," Laura said flatly. "And she's working for Martin Young."

Fallon retained his smile with a grand effort, though he was visibly upset. "I know," he said. "The enemy has sent a courier."

"I prefer the word *opponent*," Alison said.

"Nicely put. How *is* Martin?"

This was torment. She hated her great-uncle with fresh anger. "He's fine, Mr. Fallon."

"Call me Andy. Everyone does, except Laura. Andy Fallon."

"I call him Andrew," Jeff said airily.

Fallon chuckled tensely. "You were quite a boy reporter," he said. "If I remember, you even had the guts to take a poke at our friend Marty Young. Did the other kids beat you up?"

Jeff began to look worried. "No, Andrew, not yet."

Fallon laughed. The laugh echoed hollowly in the foyer. "Kids don't know who I am," he said. "I'm too old, not sexy enough. It's not my fault that my hair stopped growing."

Alison felt an overwhelming contempt for Fallon, even if

he *was* a friend of Gramps. Gramps did not behave this way.

"Well," Fallon said lightly. "Right now, I'd like to know where my room is."

"Yes," Laura blurted.

Fallon gave her a crisp glance. "As a matter of fact, I'm a little sore that Gordon hasn't shown up yet. I thought he'd be waiting.

"Gordon waits for no man," Jeff said. "Try to find Ed Ginger. He's the general factotum. Only decent guy on the premises."

Fallon looked around, plainly uncomfortable. "Well, where is he?"

Eerily, footsteps clattered on the stairs. The sound gave Alison the chills. Fallon twisted his head to look. But it was Dana Mallory who descended, in hunting clothes, gripping his rifle. Alison moved instinctively closer to Jeff. She wasn't looking at Fallon, and so was puzzled when Mallory stopped in his tracks and stared with narrowed eyes.

Then she realized that Mallory was staring at Fallon. She looked at the politician, and Fallon's face had gone white. There was a discernible trembling in his body. He moved his lips, soundlessly.

Mallory continued down the stairs, more slowly now. The tension in the room swelled. Mallory approached Fallon, and stopped a few paces from the shaken man. He smiled slowly, the smile splitting Mallory's face like a gash.

"Hello, Fallon," Mallory said hoarsely.

Fallon swallowed heavily. "I didn't know you were here."

"The feeling is mutual," Mallory said. He raised his rifle and ran two fingers along the oiled barrel. "Aren't you going to introduce me to your wife?"

"Sure," Fallon said. "Sure. Laura, this is Dana Mallory. We . . . met once before."

Mallory stuck out a hand. "Nice to know you, Laura."

Laura Fallon stared wildly at Andrew, who nodded. She let Mallory take her hand. Alison could not breathe. She waited for Laura's cry of pain, but none came. Mallory released her hand and hefted his rifle.

"See you around," he said. He turned and strode to the door, then continued outside.

Alison's mouth had gone dry. She didn't know what to say or where to go; she shared Fallon's humiliation. She avoided Fallon's eyes, and was therefore the first to see Uncle Gordon standing in a doorway.

Uncle Gordon came into the room and Fallon turned to him, a wolf attacking a bear.

"Foxworth," Fallon said, "Why didn't you tell me Dana Mallory was here?"

Foxworth eyed Fallon coldly. "It's not your business who my guests are, Andrew. I invited you. You came."

Fallon cleared his throat, desperately seeking to save face. But Foxworth wouldn't allow it. "I came for some rest," Fallon stammered. "I came for some time out . . ."

"Nonsense," Foxworth snapped. "You came because we're in business together and you're greedy. Now let's see about your room."

He turned on his heel and left the foyer, but he left it an emotional shambles. Fallon was a broken man, destroyed in a few short minutes. He would not look at Jeff or Alison. Laura looked at them, however, her eyes full of tears, blaming them.

Alison felt ill. She drew away from Jeff. "I'm going outside," she said.

Jeff nodded, and twisted his lens cap thoughtfully.

Alison needed to be alone after a strained and gloomy chicken dinner. She explored the passageways of Foxworth Hall and found a charming surprise: a library, stocked with burnished classics as well as bright new novels and works of nonfiction. The dark oak bookstacks ringed the room, and the furniture was quiet and delicate—yellow for the sofa, white for the love seat, with occasional chairs and a high manteled fireplace. It was a stuffy, silent room, and Alison settled into the love seat, curling her feet beneath her. She flipped through the pages of a heavy, lavishly illustrated edition of *Moby Dick,* not seeing the words. Her head was too full of today's mysteries. It seemed clear that Fallon had expected this business deal to be consummated here. But spending time at Foxworth's private estate invited rumors of corruption, so Uncle Gordon must have dangled a fat carrot on his stick. What?

Fallon was also the first guest with some connection to Alison. He was Martin's opponent. That might mean something, too.

She heard footsteps and looked up. Dr. Preston had come into the library. He seemed to fill the room, bulky in his clothes. He looked at Alison and settled his bulk onto the sofa. Alison tore her eyes from him, but she knew he was there. His breathing was nasal. And he hadn't chosen a book. He was just sitting, and looking at her.

She buried herself in *Moby Dick.* And now Cory Shaw was in the room. Alison knew that it wasn't coincidence. They had sought her out. Shaw moved around in front of the fireplace, and eased his lanky frame onto the love seat, a foot or so from Alison.

Alison's throat constricted. It was silly, of course. These men would not hurt her. This was her Uncle Gordon's house, and he had *promised*. Still, it was hard to shake the case of nerves that had seized her. But she could not leave; not now. It was a matter of principle.

For long moments, while a clock on the mantel ticked thunderously, it was a case of waiting for the third shoe to drop. Alison became cramped and uncomfortable. There was nowhere to look, except at the pages on her lap, and her body was becoming stiff. The two men sat wordlessly.

Dana Mallory finally arrived. Alison was almost relieved. He closed the heavy door to the library and leaned against it. She looked at him and saw steel. He launched himself into the room, which was now unbearably warm despite the air conditioning. He pulled over a chair and straddled it. Alison was effectively surrounded.

"Close the book," Mallory said.

Terror rippled through her. She bit down on her lip and turned another page. Mallory's hand struck like a cobra, ripping the book from her hands, throwing it to the carpet, where it sprawled grotesquely.

Alison stared at her empty hands, hardly breathing. She prayed silently. She could feel Mallory's breath on her cheek.

"Look up," he said.

She looked up, realizing that her eyes had filled. She didn't want that, and scolded herself. She wanted to defy them, but she didn't trust her voice.

Mallory's face was angry and impatient. "We heard some news about you," he said. "We heard you're pretty close with Martin Young."

"I'm just working for him," she whispered.

"We know that," Dr. Preston said. His voice was kind, an extension of his professional demeanor. He'd doubtless ended careers and dreams in that voice.

"The important thing," Mallory went on, "is that you're on the inside. You know Young's business."

"Not all of it," she said.

"Shut up." She recoiled, expecting Mallory to hit her. Mallory leaned closer. "I want to know what Fallon is doing here."

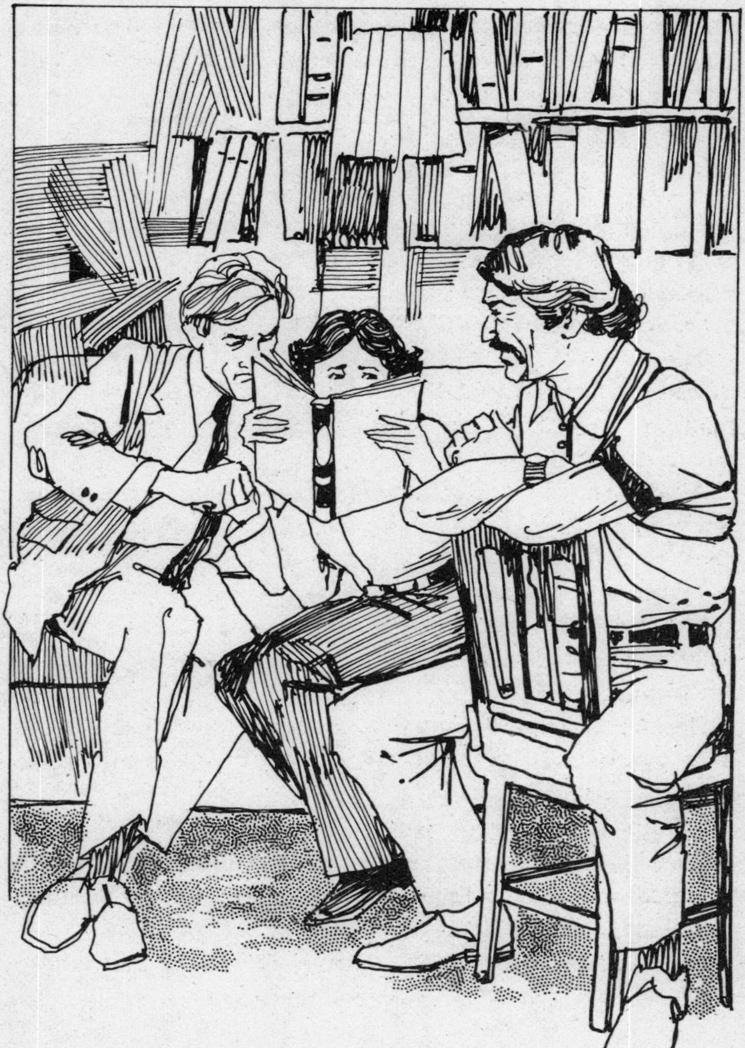

Alison forced herself to swallow. She was in the middle of a nightmare. Uncle Gordon hadn't told Gramps anything about *this*.

"I don't know," she said. "I was surprised to see him."

Mallory's hand struck swiftly. He grasped her face in his iron fingers and forced her head back. All she could see was his huge black moustache and the white of the ceiling.

"Don't play with us," he said. "We're grown men. We get invited this week. Then you come. Then Fallon. Who's next? Martin Young?"

"Let go of me."

"When I'm ready. Now I want answers. What do you know about Fallon?"

"Nothing." Her voice broke.

"Tell me."

"Dana." It was Preston's voice. "Don't get carried away."

Mallory hissed. "Don't go soft, Jonas. You have as much to lose as the rest of us."

"Hurting the girl won't accomplish anything," Cory Shaw said.

"I want answers."

"She might not know."

Mallory wrenched his hand away. "She knows. Do you think she's here by accident? If we don't make her talk, we stay in the dark. And Foxworth plays with us. Is that what you want?"

There was silence. The other man looked away.

"All right," Mallory said. "Then we work on her until she comes across. If you're too squeamish for the job, leave the room."

Alison wrapped her arms across her chest and huddled in the love seat. She considered screaming. But she could prove nothing, and she had the feeling Uncle Gordon wouldn't help her anyway. Still, she couldn't sit here and be tortured.

Mallory sat down again, seized her jaw, and twisted her head to face him. "Now, little girl, I am going to stop dancing with you. If you don't talk, I'm going to hurt you. Do you understand?"

She cried openly now. "Please," she said. "I don't know anything. Why don't you believe me?"

"I can't afford to believe you. Now, one more chance . . ."

The library door swung open. Dana Mallory turned his head with a low curse. Alison pulled free of his hand and looked. Jeff came into the room slowly, puzzlement changing to anger on his face.

"What's going on here?" he demanded.

Mallory stood, hands loose at his sides. He could have crushed Jeff easily.

"We're having a private meeting," he said. "I think you ought to leave."

"Alison, do you want me to leave?"

She wiped at her face hastily. "No," she said.

Jeff smiled at Mallory. "See? I'm wanted."

Mallory took a step toward Jeff. Cory Shaw jumped to his feet. "Dana. He's a reporter."

"That's right," Jeff said. "Pen is mightier than the sword. Peter Zenger case. All the news that's fit to print."

Mallory paused, his animal fury straining. Finally, he relaxed and swiped at the air with a disgusted hand. "Let's go," he said to the other two men.

Dr. Preston seemed relieved as he heaved his bulk from the sofa. Jeff watched the three men file out of the library, then shut the door and took a deep breath.

"Those clowns are weird," he said. "I want to tell you, I was scared."

Alison didn't trust herself to move just yet. She was shaking too hard. "Thank you," she said.

"Well, don't thank me yet. I'm not sure what I did. I was looking for you, and Ed Ginger told me there was a whole crowd in the library. I didn't expect to see Mallory beating you up."

Alison managed a smile. "He wasn't beating me up. He was threatening me."

Jeff headed for the sofa and sat. "Why?"

She looked at him, knowing her face was tearstreaked. "I don't know why. He thinks I know something about Andrew Fallon. Why Fallon is here. I couldn't figure out what he wanted."

"Rough game, politics."

She nodded, shutting her eyes briefly. "Very rough game. Gramps never warned me."

"No reason to warn you. It's not supposed to be this nasty at the senatorial level. Those men are pretty desperate. They must have something going with Fallon."

"All right," she said with bitterness. "Let them. Let them destroy each other. But I want out of it. I don't know what my great-uncle wants, but it's his problem. I didn't come here to be terrorized."

Jeff said nothing. She got up, retrieved *Moby Dick* from the floor and replaced it on the shelf. Jeff stood. She turned to him. "I'm glad you came when you did. I hope you're not in trouble."

"We're *all* in trouble, apparently," he said. "But I wouldn't sweat it too much. There's a certain amount of bluff to all of this."

"I hope you're right," she said. She shivered. "I'm going to sleep. Good night, Jeff."

"Good night," he said. He left the library first and she fought the urge to call him back.

She wished that Eric was here. But he wasn't. Nor was Dad. So she'd leave and rejoin *them,* and then her biggest problem would be telling Gramps what kind of people Fallon was involved with.

Unless Gramps already knew.

She shook off the impossible thought, and hurried from the library.

5 • A Greeting From Gordon

Alison woke groggily, and focused on her traveling clock. Seven-ten. It was Sunday morning. She had already asked the night before about going to church, but Uncle Gordon had forbidden it. So she had to settle for having private devotions in her room before breakfast.

George Murdoch had intercepted her last night en route to her room and dolefully informed her that breakfast was at eight-thirty this morning. Furthermore, Mr. Foxworth specifically requested that she be on time.

She tumbled out of bed, showered and dressed half in a daze. Outside, the weather was changing. A rough wind fluttered the leaves, and heavy clouds hemmed the glowing sky. Sunlight was intermittent. She wanted very much to go home.

She chose a flowered blouse and shorts and left her bedroom unstraightened—something that irked her—but she was already late. She wanted to see Uncle Gordon as soon as possible and ask him to have her driven back to MacArthur Airport.

The house was creakily silent, and she descended the stairs

into the deserted foyer. It was chilly here. She glanced out the big bay window, parting the curtains to do so. The lake's surface shivered in the wind and the water was deep blue. It looked frigid. The small boats rocked at their moorings. She felt suddenly deserted here, trapped and alone. She didn't want to face Mallory again, or the others.

She heard footsteps and turned, on guard. She relaxed when she saw Jeff. He smiled at her.

"Good morning," he greeted. "Sleep well?"

"More or less. A few bad dreams."

"I don't blame you. I'm afraid the dreams were my fault."

"Why?"

He approached her. "I mentioned to Dr. Preston that you were working for Martin Young."

"Well, it's not exactly a secret. Why did you say *anything?*"

"He asked. I was changing film and he sort of waddled over and said he approved of my taste in women. I told him you weren't my woman. He asked how come a good-looking guy like me couldn't win you over. I told him I couldn't fight a blazing young political star. He asked who I meant and I told him."

Alison was beginning to be exasperated. "I see."

"You have to understand. He caught me at the right time. I was feeling rebuffed and a little bruised in the ego."

"I'll bet you were." She took a deep breath. "Look, Jeff. You *are* a nice-looking guy. A *nice* guy, too. If this were college, and we went to school together, I'd go out with you. But it's not. It's my great-uncle's estate, and I'm hoping to get out of here by tonight. Then I'm flying back to D.C. and you're not. And when I rejoin the Martin Young campaign, it'll be as a *worker,* not as anything else. Is all this clear?"

His face flushed. "Yeah, it's clear."

She felt warm herself. "I'm sorry to be mean, but I'm kind

of tense, Jeff. People have lied. People I trusted. Either lied or ignored the truth. I'm a little disillusioned and a little scared, and in no mood for this kind of nonsense. Can we go to breakfast?''

Jeff let out a low whistle. "Whew. You're *angry* when you're angry."

She smiled reluctantly. "I just don't like being played for a fool." She touched his arm and smiled more genuinely at him. "Come on."

He nodded, clearly struggling against some negative emotions. They went into the dining room, where the group, enlarged now with the addition of the Fallons, ate in the usual dismal silence. Andrew Fallon sat at Uncle Gordon's right, and his wife next to him. Today, the Fallons were studiously casual—he in a knit shirt and shorts, Laura in a jumper. They still looked hot and uncomfortable. Dana Mallory sat broodingly next to Laura, his eyes shifting at the sight of the latecomers. The two seats to Uncle Gordon's left were empty. For Alison and Jeff. Dr. Preston and Cory Shaw occupied the next two.

Everybody seemed to be working on the first course. Some had plates of figs, others ate plums or drank orange juice. There was a bouquet of fresh-cut flowers in the center of the table. Jeff followed Alison to their seats. Alison found a bowl of figs before her.

"You can have something different," Uncle Gordon said.

"No," she said. "I like figs."

She did like them, and they were cold and fresh. She ate in silence, as did Jeff and the others. Today, of course, she could understand why. Once, Andrew Fallon caught Alison's eye and she held the gaze, full of anger. He dropped his eyes. The white-jacketed serving boy cleared the table and Foxworth sat back, studying the group. Alison glanced at her great-uncle. *He must be enjoying this,* she thought. Bringing these volatile people together, toying with them, holding back his purpose.

She realized that he was looking at her, reading her thoughts. She flushed. Uncle Gordon touched a finger to his moustache, then addressed the group so offhandedly that it was several seconds before everyone knew that he was making a statement.

"Listen," he said. "I asked you to breakfast at this time so you would all be together. I want to counsel patience. I know that all of you are wondering why you're here, together, at this particular time. I'm afraid I can't tell you yet. We're awaiting one further guest. When he arrives—or they, actually, since he'll be coming with friends—we'll be able to get down to business."

Alison held her breath. All eyes were on Foxworth now, some eyes openly curious, some cunning, some suspicious. Uncle Gordon smiled mirthlessly. "I assure you that I don't derive special pleasure from making you dance on a string. But, as you'll understand, it's important that you be kept in the dark to a certain extent."

He leaned forward now, and his expression changed subtly, fixing his audience. "There's one further thing. Since I've told you nothing, some of you may have your own ideas of why you, and other people, are at my house. These ideas are wrong. I promise you that. So there is no reason at all for these ideas to drive you to violence or to threatening your fellow guests. I want to remind you—and I place every emphasis on this—that you are in my home, and every one of my guests enjoys my personal protection. Any rude behavior will be punished. I mean it, Mallory."

Alison gripped her cup convulsively. Mallory's breathing was labored, frustrated. Alison thought she heard him growl, but that was probably her imagination. Jeff must have made amends by telling Uncle Gordon of last night's incident. It was the first time Uncle Gordon had shown any inclination to protect her from the dangers at Foxworth Hall.

Uncle Gordon leaned back as the serving boy brought out plates of ham and eggs. "Enjoy your day," Uncle Gordon said benignly. "The facilities of the estate are yours. Try to get along with one another."

He turned his attention to the food. Alison forced herself to look at her adversaries; at Dr. Preston, who seemed pale and disturbed by Foxworth's announcement, at Cory Shaw, who chewed bitterly, unhappy at being in this mess, and at Dana Mallory, whose face remained impassive and unyielding. She wondered if he would listen to Uncle Gordon, or how Uncle Gordon could stop him if he disobeyed.

She turned to Uncle Gordon. "Thank you," she said softly.

He regarded her dispassionately for a moment, but then his eyes took on a certain warmth. "I've put you in great danger," he said. "I apologize for it."

She smiled encouragingly. "It's over now."

His face darkened. "Oh, no," he said. "Not at all, Alison. In fact, it's only begun."

Alison rested against a tree, her hands wrapped around the trunk behind her. She watched Jeff as he continued a few steps further, the sunlight dappling his shirt. He was slimmer than Eric, older looking. Well, of course, he *was* older, so that was silly. But Jeff had a sort of lithe quality to his carriage. He'd be excellent at track or field.

The forest was hotter today than it had been yesterday. Alison had agreed to take this walk with Jeff hoping that he'd stop asking her for dates. Once they'd plunged into the woods, he'd seemed more interested in taking artistic pictures, but he'd let *her* snap a few, so she forgave him for a lot of callowness.

Jeff held his camera now, and raised his head to study the pattern of leaf and branch. His eyes were serious.

"You haven't taken a picture yet," Alison pointed out.

Jeff looked at her. "I know. Some guys clip on the motor drive and take everything, then choose the best accidents. I'm too frugal for that. I want a good shot in the first place. Then I'll shoot it to death. There's a lot of material here."

"It's a beautiful estate."

He grunted. "Yeah. Beautiful like a poisonous swamp. I agree with your plan to leave."

She pushed away from the tree. "So did I. Last night I was sure I would go. This *morning* I was sure."

"What happened? You don't really believe that Foxworth's little breakfast chat will stop Mallory?"

Alison stiffened at the memory of the library. "No, I don't believe that. I don't want those men near me again."

"Then leave."

She listened to a bird caw. "There's something funny about me, Jeff. When I'm challenged . . ."

"Quiet."

His voice was urgent. Alison touched a hand to her mouth. Jeff pointed, indicating silence with a finger over his lips. She looked, caught her breath. A few yards into the forest stood a doe. She had strayed near the path, and the wind probably carried humans' scent away. The doe took a tentative step, and raised her small, perfect head. Her ears twitched. Alison had seen deer before, but this was different. This animal was uncaptured, theirs alone to see, and incredibly beautiful.

Jeff set his camera swiftly and efficiently. He was sweating, the droplets running down the side of his face. He lifted the camera to his eye, made his final adjustments, snapped a series of pictures. The quiet *whirr* of the shutter contrasted with their whispering breath. Alison wished that she could keep the image of the doe forever.

But it was over suddenly. The wind shifted; Alison could feel the change. The doe's head shot up, her huge eyes fearful. She caught the human scent, bounded through the brush with a crash of twigs, and was gone. There was only deep, green forest where she had stood. Jeff lowered his camera, let his breath escape in a long whistle.

"Thanks," he said, wiping his face and neck. "She was a beauty."

Alison smiled, shaking a little with the release of tension. "I agree. It was exciting."

It *had* been exciting, and once again Alison was touched by the strange magic of this place. The woods, the camera, the need for absolute quiet, the suspense in getting the shots, had all framed the doe's appearance and made it significant. But it was significant even without all of it. There was a sense of tragedy here, tragedy that had flooded the earth and made it more fertile and the foliage more sadly beautiful.

Jeff said, "You started to say something. About when you're challenged."

She nodded. "You asked me why I don't go home. I'm not brave, that isn't it. No braver than anybody else."

She sat on a tree stump off to the side of the path, and Jeff leaned against the hole of a tree. It felt like midday now; the air had grown still and humid. The forest chittered with the din of birds and insects.

"Let me put it this way," Alison said. "Back at Central High, I have two friends. Well, I have more than two friends, but these two are pretty close. Cynthia Davis and Paul Cantrell. Cynthia's beautiful, really beautiful. And Paul plays the guitar. We'd eat lunch together, work on the same drama productions, on the school yearbook, go to parties together. We never want to part, but we know that soon we'll have to."

She recognized the truth in all this as she spoke, with the forest shadows deepening around her. "Paul and Cynthia gave a kind of sense to my life. It's crazy sometimes, being the Vice President's granddaughter. And even my dad—always flying around the world for the International Agricultural Foundation. My brother Eric and I get into situations that—well, that aren't normal teenage situations. And sometimes it gets lonely and scary. So having these normal friends kind of fulfilled a need for roots. Does this make sense?"

Jeff nodded, saying nothing.

She sighed. "The last days of the school year, finals week, we sat on the grass and talked about going to the lake. But like the three sisters and Moscow, we never got there. We just talked. That's what they do mostly, while Paul strums an accompaniment. They think of taking this course, or getting that job. The great issues of the day pass them by. None of them has a life plan.

"But I'm different. I always knew where I was going, what I believed, what I wanted. I got involved in all kinds of hobbies and pursuits. I had no patience with them. Then came the summer and I had time to think. Their lethargy and my hyperactivity all led to the same dark road. That spooked me. I wondered if there was really anything to me after all."

She looked up. "So I came here to get away from making decisions, to get away from looking myself in the eye. I *submitted* to Uncle Gordon's invitation. I let William crawl through every little town coming here, never suggesting a faster route. I let Uncle Gordon's staff bully me.

"And then, at breakfast, it came to me. I *am* Brad Thorne's granddaughter. I *have* seen and done special things. I *am* different from Cynthia and Paul, even though I love them both. I *can* find a direction for my life. And once I realized that, I also realized that I wanted to know what Uncle Gordon was up to, and I want a chance to tell Dana Mallory where to get off." She laughed. "Well, I don't think I'll do *that,* but—well, you get the idea."

74

Jeff stood up. "Yeah, I get the idea. You *are* a special girl, Alison."

She stood up also. "I didn't mean to sound conceited."

"You don't. You sound together."

Her throat ached suddenly. "Wish I were. But I know I'll get there." She took a deep breath. "Well. I've bent your ear mercilessly. How about the story of *your* life."

He smiled, but the first words never left his lips. Two sharp cracks echoed deep in the woods, like cherry bombs. The smile faded from Jeff's mouth. His body tightened. Alison felt a shiver pass through her.

The shots rang into silence. The leaves rustled, but there was a new, eerie calm. The birds had stopped singing. Only the insects continued to drone.

"The doe," Alison whispered.

"I hope not," Jeff said in a chilled voice. "I really hope not."

"But it was another one," Alison said bitterly. "Even if it wasn't *our* doe, it was another one. Or her fawn."

Jeff shook his head. "No. They don't shoot fawns."

"Why not?" she raged. "What difference does it make?"

Her mind would not be merciful. She visualized the doe, dropping to her knees, a gout of blood at her throat, tongue lolling to one side, the trusting brown eyes wide with terror. She imagined Dana Mallory crashing through the brush, gripping the doe's snout in his hand, the way he'd held Alison's jaw . . .

Alison stared moodily at the path. "I hate you, Gordon Foxworth. I hate you and your sick friends."

Alison nursed her anger as she walked along the path. Around the next curve, she remembered another path intersected. She briefly considered taking it, and defying Uncle Gordon and the dogs and everybody. But that was foolish fury. Besides, she realized, the other path only doubled back to the path she now trod. Typical of this mess, that even determination couldn't get her anywhere.

She stopped. She glanced back at Jeff, who nodded. He'd heard it also. Footsteps, just ahead. Alison hesitated, her legs urging her to turn back, to run. Her heart drummed. She would meet Mallory and his smoking rifle.

Jeff hurried to catch her. She walked faster, forcing her movement, and rounded the curve. She didn't see the newcomer until he was nearly upon her. He'd come from the opposite direction, on the same path.

She screamed, cut off the scream with her hand. She stared at him, shaking. It was impossible, of course. Jeff reached her, and surveyed the newcomer sadly. His eyes seemed to say that he'd expected it.

Alison lowered her hand, composed herself. "You scared me," she said. "I didn't expect you."

Martin Young grinned. "I didn't expect you, either."

Alison swallowed, unsure of her emotions. "I shouldn't really be surprised at anybody who shows up here. It's a convention."

Martin's eyes flickered. "What do you mean?"

Alison smiled. "You must have *just* arrived."

"I did, about an hour ago. Foxworth met me, took me on a guided tour. In fact, he's back at the hunter's cabin. He wanted to clean up, told me to go on ahead."

Knowing that I was in the woods, Alison thought. *Knowing exactly what path I'd take. Knowing I'd run into him.* She decided that Uncle Gordon had an ugly sense of humor.

"What brings you here?" she said.

"I'm not sure. I challenged Foxworth a year or two ago. Dared him to let me and my people spend a few days here, to prove that this was an illegal hunting preserve. He ignored me, of course. Now, suddenly, an engraved invitation. I couldn't refuse, even though it puts me on the defensive."

He seemed lost in thought for a moment, then his face brightened. "Anyway, since we're *both* here, we can map out some campaign strategy."

Why was she so nervous? "I want you to meet somebody," she said. "Jeff, this is Martin . . ."

She saw Martin's eyes and turned quickly. Jeff was gone. Anger flooded her. "How childish," she said. "Childish and stupid."

Martin cocked an eyebrow. "Did I interrupt some romance?"

"No, you did not," she said stingingly. "I'm going back to the house, if you'd care to join me."

She tramped past him, leaving him puzzled and surprised.

They hiked out of the forest together and crossed the open land to the house. Martin seemed debilitated by the walk and Alison looked at him with concern. He appeared honestly relieved when they reached the rear terrace.

"Hot today," he complained. "I never could stand the summer."

They made their way through the small maze of hallways and rooms to the foyer, where Andrew and Laura Fallon were sitting in stuffed chairs. Andrew was reading a newspaper, Laura doing a needlepoint. Alison braced for the confrontation.

Martin spotted the Fallons first, since their backs were to him. He betrayed little emotion, simply drawing a sharp breath. He glanced at Alison. "When did they arrive?"

"Two days ago."

"And the boy with you?"

"Jeff Harmon? He's a magazine reporter. He also came about two days ago."

Martin made a spire of his fingers. "The Fallons and a reporter. I should never have underestimated Foxworth."

Martin fixed a campaign smile to his lips and strode into the foyer. His voice boomed when he spoke.

"Hello, Andy," he said. He stuck out his hand.

Fallon nearly fell from his chair and Alison stifled a laugh. Fallon stood slowly, quivering at this newest outrage. Laura laid down her needlepoint, accepting the surprise. She lived with the daily expectation of betrayal.

"Very funny," Fallon said. "Very cute. Did you know I'd be here?"

"No, Andy, I didn't. But I'm delighted."

Fallon noticed Martin's hand and took it savagely. Alison experienced a new rush of admiration for Martin. He had his quirks—didn't everybody?—but he was a master in situations like this.

"And Laura," Martin said. "Nice to see you again."

Laura nodded. "Hello, Martin."

Martin perched on the arm of a chair. "Did Foxworth give you a reason?"

"Yes. I needed a rest before plunging into the campaign . . ."

"Andy, Andy, please. Spare us. Did he give you a *real* reason?"

Fallon reddened. "No, as a matter of fact, he didn't. There are others here, too, other friends of his. High-powered friends. He called us together at breakfast this morning. He told us he was waiting for one more guest, and then he'd let on to his purpose. I guess you're it."

"I guess so. Then we ought to find out soon."

"He said you were coming with friends."

Martin laughed. "That sounds ominous. I do have two friends. I came to check Foxworth out, and not just on illegal hunting. I need assistants."

Fallon straightened his newspaper. "I hope you find what you're looking for."

"I think I will, Andy."

Fallon returned to his chair and pointedly cracked open the newspaper. Martin returned to Alison. "He's hiding something."

"I don't think he knows why he's here," Alison said. "Uncle Gordon is keeping it a secret."

"Until my arrival."

"Yes. You're the last of the guests."

Martin rolled his eyes. "The last guest. Sounds rather gothic."

"This whole place is rather gothic. Where are you set up?"

"The green room," Martin said. "At least I call it the green room. I'm rooming with Ted, and Jill is in the blue room."

Alison knew Ted Roth and Jill Bennett vaguely. They were Martin's lieutenants in the campaign organization. She didn't like to think of them as such, but the image had impressed itself in her brain when she'd watched a campaign rally. Martin stood on the platform, exhorting the small crowd about the dangers of drilling for offshore oil in the Baltimore Canyon, and Ted and Jill flanked him, staring out at the people with that combined ferocity and smugness that characterized all right-hand persons. She'd conjured visions of student riots, with self-proclaimed leaders haranguing by torchlight; burning-eyed, lean despots who had supplanted stuffed-shirt dictatorship with shirtless dictatorship. And always the lieutenants, the implacable faces flanking the speaker.

It was a dumb vision to keep, of course. Martin was hardly a student firebrand. But she harbored an instinctive distrust of henchmen. Probably harked back to her fascination with British history. All those prime ministers whispering into the gullible ears of kings.

"I didn't know Ted and Jill were with you."

"As I explained to Fallon, I need witnesses and assistants if I hope to gather evidence."

Alison remembered the sound of the shots in the woods, and the doe. "I'm with you," she said. "I think Uncle Gordon needs to be exposed."

"Good. When's lunch around here?"

Alison was prevented from answering by the slam of the front door. She turned. Dana Mallory strode into the foyer, shouldering his rifle. He was grimy, grinning beneath his moustache.

"Shot a buck," he said. "Some poor doe's a widow today."

Alison balled her hands into fists. Martin smiled pleasantly and said, "Then we're in for some venison."

Mallory turned to Martin. "Not from *my* buck, mister. I'm slinging that baby on the hood of Foxworth's Lincoln and taking him home. He's mine."

Martin took two steps into the foyer. "That's a little selfish, isn't it?"

Mallory paused on the first step. "I don't see that it's any of your business."

"Very much my business," Martin said firmly. "I'm a conservationist. I'm also running for the U.S. Senate. If I get in, I'm going to make sure clowns like you can't kill deer in June on a private estate."

Mallory laughed. "Well, don't expect me to vote for you."

"No," Martin said. "I just wanted to let you know."

Mallory grunted and charged upstairs. Alison came to Martin. "There are times when I wish Gramps could see you."

Martin gazed up the stairs, then at Fallon. "Well, there's a vote for you, Andy."

Fallon scowled. "I don't court that kind of constituent."

"No," Martin agreed. "They come to you."

Fallon opened his mouth, then closed it. He made a disastrous show of returning to his newspaper. Martin flashed a secret smile at Alison and hurried up the stairs.

The word began to circulate at lunchtime: Foxworth would tell all tonight. Everybody tried to be nonchalant about it, to laugh and call the mystery stupid. But the tension was unmistakable. Uncle Gordon had gathered his prey. They'd all fallen neatly into his trap, and nobody was going to leave without knowing his purpose.

Alison swam alone in the afternoon, since Martin was busy with his colleagues. Jeff was nowhere in sight. Now and then, Alison would see Mallory, or Preston, or Shaw, alone or in concert. Whispering, gesturing. Fallon and his wife walked around the house once. George Murdoch appeared in dark doorways and frowned. Ed Ginger continued to whistle and dispense good cheer as he polished glasses. Finally, unabashed eyes glanced skyward as the sun waned and purple bands spread across the horizon. Bird cries refreshed the evening and a breeze sprang up. Uncle Gordon was making himself scarce, and did not appear at dinner, which was the most ludicrous meal to date. Nobody dared to look up from his plate, lest he risk catching another eye. The food was chalk in Alison's mouth. Jeff studiously occupied a seat at the other end of the table. Martin sat next to Alison, encased in his own thoughts. Alison bade a cordial greeting to Ted and Jill. They sat opposite her and looked sarcastic about all this. Jill was a flaming redhead, her hair long and loose, her face pale and ascetic, her body long and angular. Ted was a stocky man of thirty, with thinning hair and a creased face with a quick smile. They spoke mostly to each other, disdaining the company.

After dinner, everyone gathered in the foyer. They wandered in by twos and threes, finding seats, or pacing. Fallon sat on the sofa with Laura, twisting his hands. Mallory chewed an unlit cigar and lounged against a paneled wall. Dr. Preston sat on a chair, his hands on his knees, and glanced frequently at a clock. Cory Shaw paced feverishly. Jeff stood by the front door, holding the curtain aside and looking out. Ted and Jill stretched on a sofa, smirking and making asides to each other. Martin lit a cigarette and smoked distractedly.

Alison sat uneasily on a chair and watched Martin. He wore a worried look. She felt eerily detached, as if she were watching this on television. Gramps, and Dad, and Eric seemed part of another existence, in another time. It seemed she'd been here forever.

She probed for emotions. Fear, yes, but muted now, not overt. Somehow, she knew she was protected. She would be allowed to suffer, but only to a point.

A window-rattling growl sent the gathering into panic. Alison saw the dog first, and screamed. The dog was a shepherd, black lips drawn back over its fangs. Alison could not help noting that Mallory remained still, against the scattering of the others. Screams pierced the room.

Gordon Foxworth, dressed in black, appeared behind the dog. He spoke once in sharp command. The dog dropped to the floor, eyes lazily shut. The flurry of movement stopped; Foxworth's guests, breathing raggedly, glared at him, shocked and angered.

"There is a wall," Foxworth said without preamble. "A twelve foot wall, of solid stone, that surrounds my estate. Atop the wall is an electrified wire with a current of 1200 volts running through it. I also maintain a highly advanced security system, whose sensors will alert me long before you reach the wall. Should you feel the necessity of trying it, and even should you reach the wall, know that dogs, like Randi here, are chained every fifteen feet along the wall. And each chain is twelve feet long."

Foxworth stepped into the foyer. His eyes searched the guests. "As you know, I also have dogs guarding the paths in the forest. And the front gate, which is also electrified and protected by advanced security systems. You were brought here in my limousine for a reason. I wanted nobody with a car, in case some genius learned how to get past the gate. My sophisticated alarm system will find within minutes anybody who manages to gain the outside. On foot, there isn't much you can accomplish."

He smiled. "But I don't think any of you will try daredevil escapes. You'll have realized by now that you are prisoners."

Slowly, the shocked guests found seats, or expanses of wall, and sat or leaned. Nobody dared look at anybody else. Alison swallowed to ease her constricted throat, but she was helpless to untie the knot in her stomach.

Foxworth stood at ease, his hands behind his back. "I rarely leave Foxworth Hall," he said quietly. "When I *do* leave, it's generally for an important conference. One such conference came up the week of May 21st. Dr. Jonas Preston asked me to come to his hospital on the North Shore of Long Island. You're all familiar with the place. You were all there during that week.

"Dr. Preston, along with Dana Mallory and Cory Shaw, had a business proposition. An—investment fund, I'll call it. It looked promising. There was no reason to doubt. I've often done business with these three men. So I had William drive me to the hospital, where I met Dr. Preston and later became a guest in his home."

Alison looked at Martin and Jeff. Their faces were tense, expectant. Uncle Gordon cleared his throat before going on.

"Jeff Harmon was doing a piece on the hospital at the time. Martin Young and Andrew Fallon also happened to be in the area. They'd chosen the same week to hammer away at the money vote on Long Island. Fallon had an easier time of it, I'm afraid. They tend to be conservative on the North Shore."

He smiled to himself. "The week began well. I had preliminary meetings with Dr. Preston, and later Mallory and Shaw joined us. The deal was in our pockets. Then a strange thing happened. William was driving me from the hospital, where I'd had a late meeting with Dr. Preston, to Dr. Preston's home. The roads between the two points are dark and deserted, winding through forest for the most part. There was a bright moon that night. As we drove around a particularly steep curve, somebody took three shots at me."

There was a murmur in the room, mostly of surprise. Alison took a quick survey of faces, but she couldn't tell.

"The first shot hit the side of my car," Foxworth continued. "The second shattered the rear window, but missed me. The third missed the car entirely, as we were out of range. The closeness of the first two shots convinced me that an expert was at work. I was saved, ironically enough, by the incompetence of today's help. Morris, my old chauffeur, always kept my cars in sparkling condition, including the windows, which were cleaned daily. William is considerably more lax. Because of it, the windows were grimy, and they reflected the moonlight. To the killer's disadvantage. At least that's my theory. Maybe I was just lucky."

Foxworth looked suddenly old and tired. He made an obvious effort to bear up, to retain his vigor. But it was suddenly clear that this wasn't an easy joke for him. He was deadly serious, and he was as tense as anybody in the room. *And why not?* Alison realized. *He's locking himself in with a killer.*

"It took some juggling to get all of you here at the same time," Foxworth said. "But it's done. You're the suspects. I never reported the incident to the police because there's nothing they could have done, except to question you. To no avail, I'm sure. None of you have obvious motives. Not terribly obvious, anyway. But you *do* have motives. You know what they are. You also know if you're guilty. If you're not, you have no need to worry. Only the would-be assassin would be wise to sweat. Because in the space of one week—by Sunday, June 24th—he will have revealed himself to me, and I'll mete out his punishment. Meanwhile, continue to enjoy the estate. My house is yours."

He half-turned, then stopped. "One more thing. Alison, you're obviously not a suspect. But it's very important that you be here this week. You'll know why when the week ends. Trust me. But don't trust anybody else. Not until you're certain. I'm going to bed now. I'm not feeling well at all. Good night."

He disappeared through the doorway, calling the dog after him. For a long time after he left, there was a heavy silence in the room. Alison heard a muttered curse here and there, an exhalation of breath. Fallon spoke first.

"It's kidnapping," he said. "Simple as that. All we have to do is get in touch with the police. He must have an outside line."

"Yes, he must," Martin said sardonically. "And no doubt he'll make it available to you."

Fallon stood, circled, exhorting the group with his eyes. "Well, don't tell me you're all going to sit here and let him get away with it?"

"What choice do we have?" Dr. Preston asked.

"But it's criminal . . ." Fallon exploded.

Mallory chuckled. "Why are you so nervous, Fallon? Maybe you're the guilty party."

Fallon flushed. "Don't be stupid, Mallory."

Mallory looked calmly at his fingernails, bit a cuticle. "I'm a lot of things, Fallon. I'm lowborn, I'm uneducated. But I'm not stupid."

Laura stood timidly and placed a hand on her husband's elbow. "Drew, don't get into a fight."

Fallon subsided reluctantly, collapsing into his seat and

muttering to himself. Cory Shaw seemed paler than ever. "I can't stay here," he said. "They're after my scalp. I have to defend myself."

"What are you complaining about?" Dr. Preston snapped. "While I sit around getting sunburned, they're cleaning out my office."

"Hey," Mallory laughed. "Considering *my* problem, this is the safest place to be."

Jill Bennett shook her head. "This is a definite bummer," she said.

Jeff moved toward the stairs. "Well, prisoner or not, I have a story to write. And a writer needs his beauty sleep. Night all."

Alison watched him climb the stairs and tried to think clearly. Dad was wrong; there *was* a dark secret, and Uncle Gordon meant her to know it, so that Gramps could know it.

That Andrew Fallon was a would-be murderer?
Why?

She would probably be able to handle this in the morning. Right now, she had the urge to laugh hysterically.

But nobody else was smiling.

6 • Pursuit

The indoor pool was situated in the left wing of the house. A huge enclosure with a vaulted ceiling, the room was done in dark blue tile and white marble, accentuated with mirrors. The pool itself was nearly Olympic sized, freeformed, the water dark and clear. A glass wall looked out on the sloping lawn and the woods beyond, the view including a slice of the lake. Alison stood by this wall now, in a lime-green swimsuit.

The day was overcast. It was the dismal kind of overcast that promised days of foul weather. It had drizzled on and off this morning. Now a light wind had roiled up, tossing the tops of the trees.

Alison heard Martin splashing and diving in the pool. She glanced longingly at the lake, wanting to be there, even in this bad weather. She didn't like swimming indoors. True, Uncle Gordon had somehow managed to reduce the awful reek of chlorine, but there remained something steamy and decadent about this room. In a way, the indoor pool was at odds with the rest of the house: a sensuous perfume thrown against a woodsy after-shave.

Alison's thoughts tumbled over each other, not making sense. Today had not brought resolve. She had planned to test Uncle Gordon, to find out if she was a prisoner also, but Uncle Gordon was keeping a low profile. And she was forced to admit a certain curiosity as to the identity of his attacker.

She was also scared. This wasn't at all hard to admit. She retained a nightmarish memory of the library, and of the killer dogs. Especially of Mallory, and his omnipresent rifle. She was out of her league. *Eric should be here,* she thought.

And Eric had known that Uncle Gordon wouldn't want him.

"Hey," Martin called. "You going to stand there all day?"

She turned her head, smiled wanly. "I was thinking."

"You were striking a pose."

"I didn't mean to."

She tore herself from the glass wall with effort, wishing she could lose herself in the gray sylvan landscape. She padded to the pool in bare feet, passed the marble bench where her towel lay crumpled. She looked down at Martin, who clung to the side, treading water. His white skin glowed under the surface. His hair, plastered over his head, looked comical.

"Coming in?" he asked.

"Right now."

She jogged around to the deep end of the pool, climbed onto the diving board. She perched at the edge of the board for a moment, full of quiet exhilaration, then spread her arms and filled her lungs. She pushed herself into emptiness, saw the lapping water for an instant before she cleaved the surface. The water closed over her, much too warm to be refreshing. She kicked, torpedoed to the surface, shook her head. She swam to Martin.

"Welcome," he said.

"I wish you liked swimming outdoors," she said. "I'd have company."

"You mean the *lake?*"

"Sure."

He glanced toward the glass wall. "On a day like this?"

"Sure."

He laughed. "You're a nut."

"That's what Eric tells me." She tested the bottom and found that she could stand at this depth. "Martin, what's going to happen?"

He shrugged. "I don't know. He's a maniac, but he's got all the cards right now."

She could feel her heart beat. "What *did* happen in Westwood?"

"Who knows? Sure, I was there. In the area, anyway. I knew *he* was there also. But we never heard anything about a shooting. He must have suppressed it. If it happened at all."

"What do you mean?"

"Just what I said. How do we know he isn't making it up? A deserted road, just him and William. Foxworth tells us there were shots. That one of us did it. And everybody takes his word for it."

"Do you think he's lying?"

"I think it's possible."

"Why?"

"Well, he's got a fascinating crowd here. Friends and enemies. Which makes it hard to figure. But what would *you* do if you had all the money in the world and you wanted to get rid of somebody?"

Alison stared at him, the water suddenly clammy. "You mean kill somebody?"

"Yes. How would you go about it? If you had a private estate, guarded like Fort Knox, you might invite your victim out for a week and then arrange a timely accident. A lot of unpleasant things can happen on a hunting preserve."

"He wouldn't get away with that, Martin."

Martin laughed angrily. "Don't be naive, Alison. Men get away with murder every day. If your wallet is fat enough, you can buy justice. But still, you have a point. If *only* the victim stayed here, and then died suddenly and violently, there would be an embarrassing taint to it. Fingers would point at Foxworth. He'd have to tap dance a lot.

"But you've heard the old riddle—where do you hide an egg? With a lot of other eggs. So Uncle Gordon invites a whole gaggle of people, and then slams the gate shut. Comes up with his sad story. Lets the prisoners stew for a week, each one suspecting the other, each one scared to death that he might be unjustly accused. That's a pretty steamy situation. A violent accident can readily happen in such a crucible."

Alison saw where he was headed. "That's farfetched, Martin."

He gazed sharply at her. "Yes it is. But Gordon Foxworth is farfetched. He's a recluse, a misanthrope. He has time to think of games like this. And it's so perfect. On the last day, somebody dies. A tragic accident. Caused by the general panic. Most likely, it'll be some poor fool trying to escape. But you can rest assured that the victim will be the victim chosen by Foxworth. Gordon will appear then, repentant and grieved. He will admit to the folly of his kangaroo court. Allow the survivors to go home. Everybody so relieved to get out of this nuthouse that nobody will think twice. Now, if I could figure out who Foxworth wants erased, we might prevent it."

Alison could not make sense of it. She understood his words, but they were insane. Her great-uncle was an eccentric man, a bitter man. But not a murderer. Gramps and Dad had trusted him.

"I can't believe it," she said. "It doesn't make sense."

Martin rippled the water with his hands. "It makes a lot of

sense to me. The only thing I can't figure is you. You're the wild card. You don't fit."

"I'd be happy to go home, and solve the mystery."

He seized her arm. "Don't do that."

"Why not? I don't want to be the victim, Martin."

"I want you to stay."

The words sounded frightening to her, as frightening as this Byzantine room. Did Martin want more than just her assistance? Had she been too dumb to see it? When did *she* get to make decisions about who became more important in her personal life? She was caught now, helpless in the torrent. She knew she *would* stay, for all the reasons she'd given to Jeff, but she was terrified.

"Let's swim," she said.

The afternoon brought a steady rain, hammering at the windows, pattering on leaves and shrubs. Alison wandered perhaps unconsciously to the sunken den, which was deserted except for Ed Ginger behind the bar. She'd hoped to find him here. She paused at a narrow Tudor-style window, and looked out at the rain.

"Get you a drink?" Ed called.

She left the window and went to the bar, which Ed was polishing. "Have any orange juice?" she asked.

Ed chuckled. "Sure you can handle it?"

"Well, I'm tired. When I get going strong, you can pour me a ginger ale."

Ed brought out a glass, shook up a jar of orange juice, and poured it. "Here you go."

She drank the cold juice gratefully. "Thank you."

"Pleasure. You seem a little lost."

"I'm very lost, actually."

"Surprised to hear it. I noticed two decent-looking men chasing after you."

"That isn't the problem."

Ed leaned closer to her. "Afraid?"

She averted her eyes. "Yes, a little. No, a lot. I never expected this."

"Gordon is a lonely man. Lonely men sometimes do outrageous things. I think he wants attention."

"Martin Young thinks he wants to kill somebody."

Ed clucked his tongue. "I'd say the boy has a strong imagination. Gordon wouldn't hurt anybody."

"That's what my grandfather said. Do you really think so?"

He smiled softly. "Yes, I really think so. Is that what's bothering you?"

"It's one of the things that's bothering me. My world has been turned upside-down and I'm not sure it'll ever be right again. I count the hours now, until this week is over. That's not like me."

Ed considered. "You could probably go if you really wanted to."

She nodded. "I'll bet Uncle Gordon is waiting to see if I'll ask."

"I think he wants you here for the fireworks."

"I know."

Ed straightened. "Go ahead and be scared if you want. Perfectly healthy thing."

Alison set down her empty glass. "Do you think I'm in any danger here? Any *real* danger?"

Ed tightened the line of his mouth. Alison felt suddenly cold. "You didn't answer me," she said.

"I don't know," Ed shrugged. "I don't know what Gordon is doing, or how you fit in. I just work here."

Alison nodded. "And you agree with everything he does. Because he pays you."

"It's a living," Ed conceded.

"Even if he was going to murder somebody. You'd like to tell me about it, wouldn't you?"

Ed's face clouded. "Don't grill me, young lady."

She forced back the tears that threatened. "Don't bother to pacify me any more," she said tightly. "I don't want to make it hard on you. Or spoil your fun."

She turned and strode from the room, blindly, pushing through the hallways. She would pack her bags now, and tell Uncle Gordon she was leaving. Gramps had to know about this.

She rushed through the foyer, half-seeing the people there, not caring who they were. She plunged up the stairs and stopped at the door to her room, slightly out of breath. And frightened. She'd left the door tightly closed, but it was now ajar.

She brushed at her hair with a hand and gripped the doorknob. She pushed the door open. Andrew Fallon sat gloomily on her bed. Laura Fallon occupied a director's chair. "Who let you in here?" Alison demanded.

"We waited for you," Laura Fallon said.

"Please leave."

"We have to talk to you," Fallon said.

Alison closed the door behind her, but stayed near it. "About what?"

Fallon laughed, a short bark. "What do you suppose? What other topics are there? About your great-uncle, and about his little game."

Alison fought a fierce anger at Laura Fallon. Andrew seemed pathetic to her now, nothing more. Laura was vicious beneath her studied timidity; she assumed it was her right to go where she wanted. She regarded Alison with a bitter gaze now.

"I don't know anything about it," Alison said. "He surprised me as much as anybody else."

"I don't believe that," Fallon said. His eyes were abnormally bright. "Why are you *here*, then?"

"I was invited. I thought I'd be alone."

"Well, you're not. We're all here, and you're here. And there's a good reason for that."

"Not any more," Alison said. "I'm going home today."

Fallon stood up, shaken. "When did Foxworth tell you that?"

"He didn't tell me. I decided."

Fallon smiled slowly, settled back on the bed. "I see. Then you're not going at all."

Alison made a fist. "Yes I am," she whispered.

"Get to the point," Laura snapped at her husband.

Fallon swallowed heavily. "I wanted you to know," he said, "that I'm innocent. Completely innocent. I did not shoot at Foxworth, and I did not arrange for the shooting."

Alison stood near the bed but Fallon would not move. "I don't care," she said. "What ever made you think that I *did* care?"

"I think you care," Fallon said, a note of panic in his voice. "I think you're going to point out the one. I think your uncle brought you here to be the jury."

Alison rebelled against the words. "That's insane. I never heard of this shooting until last night."

"I believe that," Fallon said. Now he stood up. "But that's why he's going to trust you. You're unbiased. This estate is a courtroom, he's the judge and you're the jury. He's going to present his evidence all week, and he's going to ask you for a decision. And he's going to abide by it. It's the only reason he could have brought you here."

Alison sensed that Fallon was desperate. "He'd be foolish to trust me," she said.

"Not foolish. Mad. And that's precisely what he is—mad. Only a madman would concoct a situation like this. All of us, trapped here. Cooling our heels for a week while he decides which one of us took a shot at him in the dark. And then, at the end of the week, one of us is punished. Punished how? By those dogs, I'm sure. Torn to pieces. And it could be me, as well as anybody else. It could be anybody he chooses. But if you convince him that it wasn't me, he'll let me go. I don't care who else dies. Do you understand?''

Fallon was nearly in tears. Alison trembled visibly. "Get out of here," she pleaded. "Both of you."

Fallon shoved a finger under her nose. "Tell him," he husked. "Tell him that I didn't do it. I want to get out of here alive."

Alison turned away. Laura stood easily, a frosty smile on her lips. "She got the message."

Alison heard them leave the bedroom, heard the door open and shut. She sobbed once, then yanked open the top drawer of the triple dresser. She began stacking her clothes neatly on the bed, then went into the bathroom and gathered her makeup. She dragged her suitcase from the closet, lifted it onto the bed. The rain had stopped outside and the clouds scudded across a fitful sky. Alison glanced out the window, at the wild forest, at the frothing lake. She left the suitcase and went out of her room, carefully closing the door behind her.

Her head felt feverish as she hurried down the stairs and through the foyer, stepping outside into a warm, rushing wind. The air itself was stormy. She stood for a long time on the portico, then walked, head into the wind, to the rear of the house and began crossing the distance to the forest. It had struck suddenly, this need to be outside, to think clearly. As she'd emptied her drawers, a horror of leaving had overwhelmed her. She *couldn't* leave. It was insidious, nightmarish. Somehow, all of this mystery was tied up with her, in ways that Gramps and Dad and maybe even Uncle Gordon hadn't imagined. But she couldn't find the key.

Fallon was wrong. No, Fallon was a coward, and his wife only encouraged him. Uncle Gordon had never asked help from anybody, even in his lowest moments. But Fallon was terribly worried.

Now she was at the edge of the forest. The trees bent and groaned and dead leaves skittered across the path. She breathed deeply, moved into the woods. Thunder rolled in the distance. She looked up, automatically, searching the masked sky for lightning. One wasn't supposed to be in the woods in an electrical storm.

She remembered the dogs, and stopped. But this was her path. Uncle Gordon had chosen it for her. She stepped gingerly, her breath rasping in her throat. Now she saw the dogs, pacing nervously. They looked at her, tongues lolling. She trembled the length of her body. She forced herself to continue, and passed among the dogs. Beyond them, she broke into a relieved jog, then a run, her breath heavy on the silence.

She slowed to a walk, coated with perspiration. Here it was calm and windless. The day darkened. She would miss dinner. But she needed to go on, to penetrate more deeply, to invite . . . what? Was she asking for attack, for a confrontation? She knew now where she was heading, but what would she find there?

There was stillness now, a humid lull, punctuated by the drip of sap or of rain, she couldn't tell which. She sensed her aloneness, felt the awful weight of trees pressing down on her, of deadly things that lay beyond the path. Soon, there would be the hunters' cabin. Around the next bend, or the bend after that. She'd forgotten the distances.

She was thinking of Martin now, remembering him in the pool; the whiteness of his skin against the sickly water, the wetness of the tiles, the cold marble. And Martin's decayed, ghoulish words. His accusations. The pool seemed brackish in her memory now, and she recalled Martin's eyes being unnaturally bright. Everything here took on the aspect of dark fantasy. People were seen in a new light, the weird half-light of the forest, a light that came from no sun or moon, but from the haze of the forest itself—a milky web hung between black trunks, a chittering of hidden creatures.

She found it hard to breathe, unbearably humid. This was foolishness. She would find nothing in the hunters' cabin. She had to go home. She had to turn back.

She stopped and listened. A twig cracked. An animal. But now there was a steady tread: shoes, crunching leaves, not caring about being heard. On the path behind her.

In her mind she saw Mallory and his rifle. She saw Laura Fallon, holding a small handgun. Smiling, always smiling.

She ran, horrified to find her legs exhausted. She threw back her head and drew in burning air, pushed on. Now the feet behind her ran also, and she knew she was being chased.

She cried out softly, afraid and angry. If she could reach the hunters' cabin . . .

She shut her eyes, gasping as a stray branch cut her over her eye. She flailed, looked again, saw blurs. She could not go on. She had a few yards left in her, no more. Then she would fall and her pursuer would reach her.

She fell against a tree, her lungs on fire. She listened with morbid fascination to the rasp of her breathing. She listened for her pursuer, but she heard nothing. He must have stopped, or taken a wrong turn.

She made herself stand, stumble ahead. The woods looked strange to her: tapestries of trees, mist-filled gullies. The hunters' cabin had to be a few feet ahead.

She listened to the drumbeat of her heart as she walked, pushing one foot in front of the other. Once in the cabin, she would phone the main house and ask for Uncle Gordon. Tell him that she was being pursued, and would he come for her?

Inform him that, once safe, she wanted to go home.

She held the thoughts as she staggered around a curve and heard phantom footfalls. There was something dreadfully wrong. It couldn't have been this far. She'd been walking for hours, it seemed. And the forest was horribly dark, a bluish mist permeating the milky color. The trees were disappearing in night, a high wind creaking in the upper branches. She'd missed supper, she knew that. It hurt to think about that, and she foolishly began to cry.

Her wits returned when she saw light through the trees, a distance away. Enough light to indicate a clearing, where the cabin stood. She brushed grime from her face and shivered. She had a bad thought. Suppose her pursuer had gotten there first . . . but that was impossible. He would have had to crash through dense forest.

She moved ahead, finding now that she could run slowly and clumsily. But the strength was there for this last exertion. She was a little worried about herself. She always kept in shape, exercised, ate well—there was no reason to be this tired this quickly. It had to be the excitement.

The light loomed closer: a blue light, the light of dusk. And other lights, much further away, blinking white through the trees. She wondered in the back of her mind. What had Uncle Gordon said about keeping the hunters' cabin lit at night? He'd turned off the lights when they'd left. He kept it dark.

Then what light had she seen?

A warning shot through her brain, but too late. The horrid growls assaulted her ears and the dogs were inches from her, dragging their chains, teeth bared. She stared fixedly at the glowing eyes, thought she heard herself scream.

She was suddenly out of their reach, but a stab of pain ripped through her wrist. She slammed against a tree trunk, and the dogs were leaping, straining at their taut chains. She must have jumped back. Now she cowered against the tree, making small frightened noises in her throat, trying to understand.

The shots brought her out of it. She straightened. A second volley of shots rang through the woods, and she heard a cry. She stared around, trying to locate the source of the gunfire, but the snarling of the dogs blocked out other sounds.

She knew she had to escape, distraught though her mind was. She turned, took several steps back into the forest, and pitched forward as darkness overwhelmed her.

7 • First Victim

She was aware first of extreme cold. Her limbs came awake individually, shocked at the hard bed on which she sprawled.

The low growls of dogs brought her around. She remembered that she was in the woods, at Foxworth Hall. She remembered blundering through the forest, coming upon the dogs, falling. She shivered now in the evening chill. She raised her head.

There was nothing to see. Darkness had fallen utterly. The invisible forest was alive with the humming of insects and the tread of animals. She thought she saw burning eyes peering at her from the brush. Shakily, she dragged herself to a sitting position. The earth was very cold.

Fear spread slowly, as wakefulness came. She could not see the path three feet in front of her. She'd never find the other path, the safe one. She'd probably become lost in the forest. Yet, she couldn't cross the few yards to open ground without being torn apart by the dogs. She had no choice at all.

She brushed wetness from her cheek, angrily. She'd gotten

herself into this mess, she would get herself out. If she waited until her eyes adjusted to the darkness, she would be able to make out the path.

She heard footsteps now, very close, and very cautious. And she saw a beam of light flaring among the trees. She went rigid, praying that the searcher was friendly.

The footsteps were closer, the beam of light now constant as it flashed between branches. The searcher waved the flashlight back and forth, covering the path and the brush on either side. She watched, barely breathing. It was eerie that he did not call out to her.

Now he was in sight. A man of medium height, somewhat stooped. The flashlight caught her eyes and she winced, throwing up a hand to ward off the glare. The man stopped, held the light on her.

"Please," she begged.

The man came closer. Alison tried to stand, was amazed to find herself too weak. The man stood over her now, and lowered the flashlight to his side. She looked up at him, her faced streaked with tears from the pain of the light.

The man glared down at her with old, sunken eyes. The gnarled face and body identified her rescuer: George Murdoch.

"Hi," she said weakly. "Glad you came."

She reached out a hand for him to assist her, but he only watched. She grimaced, retracted the hand.

"I can't get up," she said. "I'm too weak. Can you help me?"

"I found ye," Murdoch growled. "That's enough."

"Thanks," Alison said. "You must have read Dale Carnegie cover to cover."

There were more footsteps now, much firmer and more resolute. And another waving beam. And suddenly, there was a strong voice.

"Alison? Murdoch, did you find her?"

Alison's heart flipflopped with relief. "Uncle Gordon," she said hoarsely.

The footsteps pounded now, a man running. Uncle Gordon loomed out of the darkness, aimed the flashlight at her. She shut her eyes, then the glare was gone.

"Thank God," he breathed. "Murdoch, why didn't you call out?"

"Ye were right behind me," Murdoch said.

Uncle Gordon expelled a long breath. "Are you hurt, Alison?"

"I don't know. I can't seem to get up."

Uncle Gordon dropped to one knee, and his proximity was comforting. He examined her cursorily, put pressure on parts of her body. He made a small grunt of satisfaction.

"I see the problem. You fell on your leg. It's probably numb. I'll get you up and you can walk it off."

He stood, gripped her hand, and she was pulled to her feet with the lightness of a feather. She nearly fell again, and realized that she had no sensation in her left foot. Uncle Gordon supported her and she stepped down with the dead foot until a tingle passed through her thigh. After several minutes, feeling returned enough to walk sloppily.

"Ready to go back?" Uncle Gordon asked.

She nodded.

He took her hand, threw an arm across her shoulders and led her past the docile shepherds, Murdoch following. They crossed the open ground, and Alison watched the lights of the house grow closer.

She was taken to the library, eased onto the love seat. The room made her tighten. She realized that she was rather bedraggled. Uncle Gordon sat beside her.

"You gave me a scare," he said. "You're also bleeding."

She started at that. He held her left wrist. She saw the gash now, the rivulet of blood. She remembered the attack of the dogs.

"My animals are quite healthy," Uncle Gordon said. "No chance of infection. Still, we should dress that."

The next moments passed confusingly. She was alone, then with Uncle Gordon and Ed Ginger, as they returned together. She winced at the sting of antiseptic, relaxed as they applied the bandage. Ed Ginger hurried out, and Uncle Gordon remained.

"You'll want to get cleaned up," he suggested.

"Yes. I could use a shower."

There was a taut silence. Uncle Gordon's eyes were far away now. "What happened, Alison?"

"I was being followed. I ran. I must have blundered onto the wrong path."

"Exactly. And you forgot about the dogs?"

She shook her head. "No. I was confused. I thought I saw the hunters' cabin, but it was the house. I'm sorry."

At least it explained why she was so exhausted and why the walk had taken so long. She'd doubled back to the house on a much longer path.

"Don't apologize," Uncle Gordon said. "I can understand why you were tense."

Suddenly, she remembered the last sound she'd heard, before her collapse.

"The shots . . . who was shot?"

"I don't know yet. We're searching for the victim. We should find him soon."

Alison leaned her head back against the love seat. She was clearheaded now. She knew she wouldn't run foolishly into the forest again.

She studied Uncle Gordon. This was the first time she'd had the opportunity to see him, to be alone with him. His face was impassive now, the deeply etched lines a map of his own private suffering. He was an educated man, a man of letters and culture. He could manipulate the English language with grace. He was conversant with the arts, with politics, with business. And he was slightly paranoid. "Uncle Gordon," she said, "is this what you wanted? People getting shot?"

He gave her a cryptic smile. "Don't judge me yet, Alison."

"I'm not judging. I'm trying to make sense of things. I was going to ask you to take me home today."

"I would have said no."

The words surprised her. She stifled a flicker of fear. "No?"

"That's right. I want you to stay the week."

"I can tell Gramps and Dad about this when I go home."

"I hope you won't. Not all of it."

"No—you're *sure* I won't. Why?"

"Why not live out the week?"

The anger came boiling to the surface, spilling out. "I'd like to live out the week, Uncle Gordon. But there seems to be a distinct possibility that I won't. George Murdoch forgot to tell me about the dogs the day I came. You didn't seem very upset, I've been stalked and harrassed and threatened. It's not my idea of a vacation."

"Nor mine," Uncle Gordon said. He dropped onto the couch, looking smaller. "But all moments in our lives are not frivolous."

"But my summer *is* frivolous," she said. "I just finished my junior year in high school, and I have some time off. Only a little, because I'll be working for Martin Young. I'd like to loaf around for a while. Like a normal sixteen-year-old. I don't mind big estates and dotty uncles, but I don't like nightmares."

She was on the razor edge of exhaustion and knew it. Uncle Gordon's eyes hardened. "If this week is your toughest sledding in life, you're a lucky girl, Alison. But it gets nastier. There are Mallorys in the world. They're not nice, and you have to deal with them. You know that. You've met nasty customers. It's time you learned how to bear up under adversity."

"Like *this?* And if Mallory had beaten me here the other night, would that have proved something?"

"I'd have repaid him."

She stared wildly at him. *"Repaid* him? And let me take a beating?"

"Yes."

She seethed. "You're a sick man, Uncle Gordon. You've suffered, and I sympathize with that. But you're not God. You can't inflict your moral lessons on others. I'll take my own beatings in life; I don't need to have them arranged by you."

Uncle Gordon fidgeted. "You're a very articulate girl, Alison. I'm happy to see that. Few young people can communicate now."

"Don't change the subject," she said. "You always change the subject when it gets too hot. You kidnapped me, Uncle Gordon. Let's use plain language. You're holding me prisoner here and you've put me in danger. Of my life. If I get out of here in one piece, I'm going to make sure the authorities come down on you, hard. You can't walk around like a petulant little boy, breaking toys because your dog died."

Uncle Gordon went rigid and Alison quailed at the strength inside the man. He said nothing for a long time. When he did speak, the words were measured and restrained.

"Yes," he said. "You're in danger, Alison. Of your life. Like every one of my guests. If you learn how to survive, you'll make it. If not, you'll die. That's your problem for the week. What you do afterward to me is my problem. I'm not worried."

Ed Ginger filled the doorway suddenly and Alison turned to him, sensing at once that disaster had struck.

"We found the shooting victim," Ed told them. "It's Martin Young."

Martin was not alone in the foyer when Alison and Uncle Gordon arrived. Dana Mallory and Cory Shaw had come to see what the commotion was, and Andrew and Laura Fallon were descending the stairs. Ted and Jill sat together, looking amused.

Martin sat on a side chair, his shirt off. Dr. Preston had a first-aid kit spread out on a pedestal table, and was cleaning an ugly wound in Martin's right shoulder. Preston tossed a bloody piece of cotton into a paper bag and took another, dipping it in peroxide.

Martin winced, turned his head and saw Alison. He managed a weak smile.

"Foxworth," he said. "When you open a hunting season, you do it right."

Alison went to Martin, looked at him. "How are you?"

"Mostly scared," he said.

"Very lucky boy," Dr. Preston muttered. "Bullet just creased the shoulder."

"So we have to look for a sloppy marksman," Martin said.

"Don't joke," Alison admonished. "I was in the woods. I heard the shots."

"I know you were in the woods," Martin said. "I was following you."

Alison stared at him. "You? Why didn't you call out?"

"I'd have felt silly. I figured I'd catch up with you in a minute or two. But you outfoxed me."

"I thought I was being chased. I turned onto the wrong path. Uncle Gordon found me."

Martin looked grim. "It's a wild night in the forest."

Uncle Gordon examined Martin's wound quickly. Dr. Preston finished dressing the shoulder and Martin flexed his arm, grimacing.

"It'll be stiff for a while," Preston told him.

Martin rested his hands in his lap. Despite his jaunty demeanor, he'd been badly jolted. He looked terribly vulnerable now, and scared.

Uncle Gordon surveyed the room as the guests milled about, staring at the casualty. Mallory lit a cigar very calmly.

"This kind of throws everything into a cocked hat," he said. "I figured they'd be gunning for *you,* Gordon."

"They might have been," Foxworth said. "In the dark, Mr. Young may have been mistaken for me."

Mallory laughed harshly. "By a marksman? Come on, Gordon. You said the guy who shot at you was a pro."

"Yes," Foxworth said. "But he might have been a hired pro. And his boss might be a lousy shot, but desperate. And there's another possibility, Dana. If you were a marksman, and you wanted to kill a man, you'd have to figure they'd come to you first when the man died, right?"

Mallory chewed the cigar. "Sounds good."

Foxworth approached Mallory deliberately. "Well, then, you'd want to cover your tracks. In advance. If you shot up a few other people first, made yourself look like a real fumbler, then once you hit your intended victim, nobody would look for you. How does that sound?"

"Dumb," Mallory said.

Ed Ginger had been standing in the doorway for a while. Now Foxworth noticed him. "What is it, Ed?"

Ed looked at the guests. "I checked the racks in the gun room," he said. "There's a rifle missing."

A murmur rippled through the gathering. Foxworth turned to Mallory. "How about it, Dana?"

Mallory spat out a piece of cigar. "I never went to the gun

room," he said. "I have my own weapon, and I keep it in my room. You know that, Gordon."

"But you wouldn't use your own weapon for a job like this."

Mallory's jaw tightened. "I didn't take the gun, Foxworth."

Foxworth studied Mallory's face for a moment, then turned his attention to the others. "I'll require excellent alibis from everybody."

Dr. Preston was sweating heavily. He rubbed his pudgy hands together. "I was playing cards with Cory in the library."

"That's right," Shaw seconded. "Blackjack and gin."

Foxworth glanced at both of them. "Convenient. You'll back each other up. Except that I don't trust either of you."

His glance fell on Andrew Fallon, who commenced shaking at once. "I was upstairs with my wife," he stammered. "We were about to undress for bed."

"But you didn't undress," Foxworth said.

"We're adults," Laura said chillingly. "I didn't know we had a curfew."

Mallory moved away from his favorite wall, easing his frame across the room. "This is pretty funny," he said. "Foxworth grilling us. We're forgetting something. He's the one who trapped us all here. He's the one who thinks one of us tried to kill him. He's the one with the most to gain by knocking us off—one by one. Maybe starting with Martin Young, then turning us on each other."

Dr. Preston set his mouth. "That's right, Foxworth. You're the organizer of this little party. Where were *you* when Young was shot?"

"Good question," Cory Shaw echoed.

The murmur turned ugly, and swelled. Alison held her breath. Uncle Gordon faced the guests squarely, and didn't appear worried. "It's possible," he said. "Except that I'm the best shot here. If I wanted to kill Martin Young, I wouldn't have missed."

"No?" Mallory pointed to Foxworth. "I thought I heard you say something before. About a man who can shoot. Who wants to kill a guy. How he might foul up. And Foxworth, you have every reason for wanting to get rid of Martin Young. He's out to scalp you—he wants to take this estate from you and give it to the slobs out there for a park. You got to hate him for that."

Mallory's eyes grew bright now, and the others hung on his words. "Maybe we've all been looking at the ends of our noses, and no further. Maybe Foxworth was lying, and nobody took a shot at him. Maybe he's scared of Martin Young winning the election, and he figured a foolproof way of killing him. Sure, one miss. Makes it look good. When's the next try, Foxworth?"

Foxworth blinked, sweating gently. Mallory was a very good demagogue, Alison decided. He'd turned the others around in a matter of minutes. Each one of the guests saw an opportunity for escape. Alison was afraid for her great-uncle, but inside her, ugly and insistent, was the question: could Mallory be right? She hardly knew Uncle Gordon. Clearly Gramps had misread him. He was a man who'd lost what he loved and retained only his estate, his few acres where he could retreat from life. Now Martin threatened to take that retreat from him. It might be sufficient motive to kill. How ironic, if Martin's theory was right, and Martin was the victim.

"I don't like your accusations," Foxworth said.

"We don't like your game," Mallory retorted.

Uncle Gordon took a step or two, Mallory after him like a fanged predator. The guests surged forward. Alison caught her breath, moved closer to Martin.

The front door crashed open, ripped by the wind. Heads turned. Alison realized that one guest had been absent through all of this, so far from being a suspect that he was not even missed. Jeff entered the foyer, his shoes tracking mud from the forest floor. He gripped a rifle in his right hand.

He closed the door behind him, a little puzzled at the concerted stare. Ed Ginger strode through the foyer and wrested the rifle from Jeff's hand. He examined it quickly.

"This is the missing weapon," he said to Foxworth.

"Loaded?" Uncle Gordon asked.

Ed nodded.

Jeff licked his lips. "I stumbled onto your gun room," he said. "I was scared. There were footsteps outside my room, and somebody tried my door. I figured if there's a killer loose, I wanted protection. So I took one of the rifles, and some ammunition."

He looked frightened at his own deed. Gordon Foxworth approached him slowly. "You were in the woods tonight."

Jeff nodded. "I was looking for Alison. I wanted to talk to her. I saw her go into the woods, and I followed her."

"With the gun?"

"Yes. I was nervous about going into the forest in the dark. And it was getting dark then. I searched for her, but she'd disappeared. I got onto the wrong path and it took me until now to find my way back. You only allowed me one path where I wouldn't be killed by the dogs."

Dana Mallory pulled at his moustache. "Hey, reporter. Did you hear any shots?"

"Yes. I heard them."

"I was hit," Martin said. Jeff looked at him.

"Did you see who did it?"

"Why?" Mallory taunted. "You worried?"

Jeff glared at him. "No, curious. Didn't anybody ask him if he saw anybody?"

"No," Alison said. "No, everybody was too busy trying to accuse Uncle Gordon. It seemed easier that way."

Mallory arched a finger at Alison. "You're in no position to talk, girl. You're blood."

"That's enough," Uncle Gordon said. "Martin, Jeff is right. Did you see anybody?"

Martin shook his head. "No. I heard a shot and I ran a few steps. Then I was hit, and I fell. There were more shots. I waited for a long time before I tried to get up. But I never saw anybody."

Uncle Gordon sighed. He regarded the group dully, through tired eyes. "All right," he said. "I did not shoot Martin. You can take that or leave it. It seems fairly obvious that our guilty party is trying to cover his tracks. As I said, I expect him to reveal himself by the end of the week. It might be sooner. I suggest you all get a good night's sleep, and lock your doors."

He turned and left the foyer abruptly. Ed Ginger peered around, and then followed him. Dana Mallory laughed, a low, nasty laugh.

"He's playing us for fools," he said. "And he gets away with it."

Martin turned to Mallory. "As long as there are two sharpshooters," he said, "there's a shadow of doubt."

Mallory's facial muscles twitched in restrained anger. He looked at Martin for a long moment, then turned and headed upstairs. His exit was a signal. Muttering, the others wended their way upstairs, Cory Shaw first, then Fallon and Laura, with backward glances. Dr. Preston looked at Martin's arm again.

"Try not to move it too much," he said.

Martin nodded. "Thanks for the first aid."

Dr. Preston smiled. "I think Foxworth has us all here for a purpose. And *not* the one he's mentioned."

He crossed the foyer and climbed the stairs ponderously. Jeff was gone. Jill and Ted had not moved from their seats. They regarded Martin and Alison lazily.

"This is going to be an easy campaign," Ted said smoothly.

Martin laughed sourly. "If we survive."

Jill stood, sylphlike and sarcastic. "If you give guns to little boys, they'll shoot."

Ted laughed and hauled himself to his feet. "I'm bedding down," he said. "I think it's safer right now."

Martin grinned. "Very wise."

Alison watched Ted and Jill disappear up the stairs. They had no personalities, those two, except as extensions of Martin. They were arms.

Martin stood, swayed a bit. "Weaker than I thought," he said.

"Are you hungry?" Alison asked. "I'm starved."

Martin shook his head. "I just want to sleep. This took a lot out of me."

Alison studied him. "I don't believe Uncle Gordon wants to kill you," she said.

"Somebody does."

"It might have been an accident."

Martin raised an eyebrow. "Whose side are you on?"

"Your side."

He smiled coldly. "You get some sleep too, Alison. I have the feeling it's going to get worse before it gets better."

He shuffled through the foyer and pulled himself up the stairs as she watched. She despised herself for her coldness toward him. She was working with him, and he'd been shot tonight. Almost murdered. But no tears, no proper hysteria. Only a solicitous word or two. She'd tried to draw further emotion from herself, but she was tapped out.

The foyer seemed huge now, the paneled walls draped in

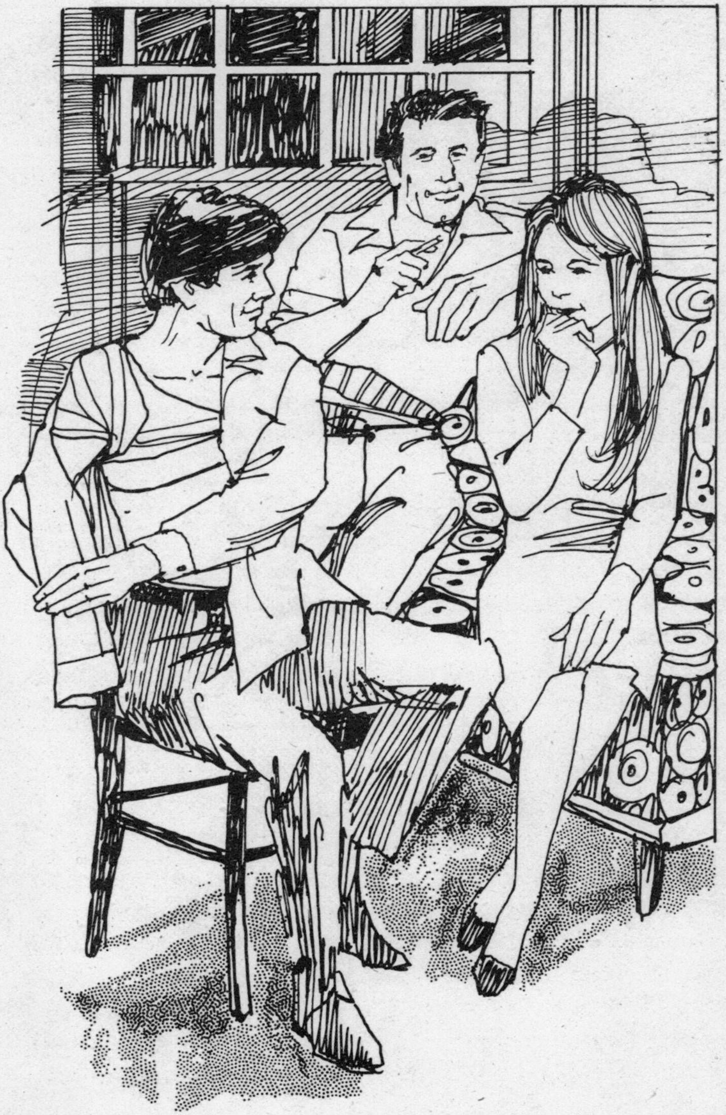

shadow. It was incredible that a few moments earlier, the room had been the scene of blood and consternation, of a dark kangaroo court with no clear defendant, no single prosecutor. The events of this evening already assumed their own unreality. Alison knew they had happened; her bones ached, and her wrist burned now with a fierce pain under the bandage. She could relive, in her mind, each of the terror-filled moments. But none of it made sense.

She turned at a sound. Jeff was framed in a doorway. She made no attempt to force down the surge of affection that rose inside her. It troubled her; she'd never thought of herself as capricious in matters of the heart. But she was too tired to fight.

"Ed Ginger is making some hamburgers," Jeff said hoarsely. "Want to join me?"

She nodded. "Yes. I can smell them."

Jeff came to her slowly. His face looked strained. "I'm a suspect, I guess."

"You came in at the wrong time."

"I stole a gun," he said. "I've never stolen anything in my life. Or shot anything. I couldn't aim if I tried. But I was nervous, and the guns were there. Unlocked."

A tremor raced through her. "Unlocked?"

"Yes, or course. How else would I manage it? I can't pick a lock. It seemed suspicious to me, too. But it's pretty clear that one of the guests is a dangerous character. I wanted to even the odds a little."

"And now?"

He laughed. "I don't want to see the dumb thing again. I was afraid of it when I held it. I would have gone into cardiac arrest if I'd had to fire the thing."

So charming, she thought. *So ingenuous. And maybe he's a smooth, capable liar.*

"Well," she said. "Let's go have those hamburgers."

He nodded. Then he noticed her hand. "How did *that* happen?"

"The dogs."

Jeff smiled. "Are you *sure* Foxworth is related to you?"

"Not only that," she said seriously. "But I think he likes me."

"With friends like *him*, . . ."

She laughed quietly and walked with him from the foyer. But neither Jeff's amiability or Ed Ginger's hamburgers could soothe her fears now.

8 • *Sitting Duck*

Tuesday dawned a thoroughly depressing day. Alison was aware of the rain long before she awakened; the insistent clatter of it on the roof pressed into her subconscious, affecting her dreams. When she finally rose through the layers of sleep, she identified the sound and squirmed deeper into her pillow. This was a day to sleep, to waste while the rain fell.

But slowly, the real terrors of her situation forced her to open her eyes, to lie staring at the ceiling. She heard movements elsewhere in the house, and she turned to check her bedside clock. Eight-thirty. It was too early to get up.

She tried to accept recent events. She visualized Martin, wounded; visualized Mallory grilling her, the dogs leaping for her throat. The thought reminded her of her injury, and she realized that her wrist had been throbbing. She held her arm in front of her eyes, and her wrist seemed to be swollen under the bandage.

She was completely awake now, and she sat up in bed. The rain sounded fearsome outside. She couldn't shake the anguish in her chest. The nightmare simply did not end.

She thought of Gramps and Dad, and Eric. Of Paul and Cynthia. Of the people she knew back home, the people she loved. Of sunny days and barbecues. She stopped herself, knowing that she would cry.

Anyway, thinking of barbecues made her hungry. She left her bed, washed and dressed, straightened the room. She opened her door, half expecting to find wild dogs in the hall. She found only silence, and gray emptiness. She glanced at the door to Jeff's room, further down the hall, and wondered afresh about the brash young reporter. It was easy to like Jeff, just as easy to be annoyed with him. He troubled her.

Dana Mallory occupied the foyer alone. He sat on a sofa with his legs crossed, and his eyes wandered lazily to Alison as she descended the stairs. She was scared, as she'd been when passing the dogs. Mallory said nothing, and did not change his expression, but she feared him. He was not simply an ignorant bully. He knew how to manipulate people, and he was capable of taking the situation at Foxworth Hall into his hands. And she was not his favorite guest.

She hurried to the dinning room, where Andrew Fallon sat at the table, picking at two fried eggs. Alison sat quietly, and the serving boy brought her a glass of grapefruit juice.

"Thank you," she said, but the boy just left. She turned to Fallon.

"Uncle Gordon must pay them to keep quiet," she said.

Fallon glanced up at her haunted eyes. It was obvious that he hadn't slept well. He returned to his eggs, not bothering to answer her. Alison drank her juice hastily.

She also had eggs for breakfast, with sausages and toast, but she ate lightly. Fear tightened her stomach and dulled her appetite. She wasn't certain she would make it to the end of the week. And what if the culprit had not revealed himself by then? Would Uncle Gordon imprison them for another week? For the entire summer? Eventually, Dad would call, and when he received no answer, he would come out. With federal agents.

And would Uncle Gordon start shooting?

Alison trembled and forced herself to quit thinking along those lines. She was getting into destructive fantasy, which was no good.

She paused, with a bite of sausage in her mouth. She had never thought of taking an active role in this strange week. But she thought of it now. There had to be a way out of the estate, despite what Uncle Gordon said.

She left the dining room, and the morose Fallon, and found others in the foyer. The rain was having the effect of intensifying the strain. Dr. Preston and Cory Shaw had joined Mallory, and were talking in low whispers. Jeff was still upstairs, and so was Martin, but Jill and Ted had come down, in dungarees, and lounged near a window, eyeing the storm with heavy-lidded eyes.

Martin made an unexpected entrance from a doorway, rather than from the stairs. Heads turned as he came in and sized up the group. Alison saw the rifle in his hand.

"I didn't steal this," Martin said. "Gordon Foxworth gave me permission to carry it. Since somebody here is out for my skin, I intend to protect myself. I just wanted everyone to know that I have the gun and I'll use it."

He found a chair and sat, the gun across his lap. Alison felt unreasonably annoyed. He was being showy. She went to him, sat in another chair close to him.

"How do you feel?" she asked.

"It hurts."

She bit her lip. "I'm sorry."

"Well, I was lucky. How's *your* injury?"

"Painful."

"We fouled up in that forest. If I'd called out to you, we'd have been together and probably escaped with a whole coat."

She nodded. "We'd better call out from now on."

He looked at her. "You seriously intend to go into the woods again."

She twined her hands in her lap. "I was thinking of it. I want to see if there's any way out."

Martin laughed sardonically. "I don't think Gordon was lying about his precautions. Do you know how to breach an electrified stone wall guarded by killer dogs?"

Frustrations rose like gall in her throat. "No, but I can't sit still and do nothing."

"None of us like it here, Alison. But for now, we have to play his game."

"Yes, for now. But what about later? He can keep us here forever if he wants to."

"People know where I am. And where Fallon is, and those three millionaires in the corner. Gordon won't risk that kind of publicity."

"But he *knows* that *some* of us will talk when we get out."

"Maybe," Martin conceded. "But then we'll all be gone, and who can prove anything?"

He studied the rifle for a moment. He hadn't shaved this morning, and he looked haggard. He seemed a stranger to Alison, not at all the driving man she'd known. It was as if they'd just met.

"How do you feel about me?" he asked suddenly.

She was caught off guard. "I don't know what you mean."

"Well, I wasn't being that subtle. Do you like me?"

"Yes, of course."

"Don't be obtuse. Back home, when I took you to dinner, that was a declaration."

She felt chilled inside. "I didn't take it that way."

He turned to look at her now. "I know you didn't. I don't think you knew that I regarded you as more than a campaign worker, and I don't think you want to know. I think you honestly believe in what I say and that kind of genuine feeling wrecks me."

She was bitterly quiet, studying her hands with great concentration. Thunder rolled outside. She could hear his breathing, and traced the patterns of his aspiration.

"You're not answering," he said, and the hurt was clear in his tone.

"I don't know what to say," she admitted.

His nearness was oppressive. "I didn't think so. I can get over not winning you, Alison. With difficulty. But you should learn some lessons. If you're going to prefer another guy, do it gracefully. Don't adore him openly when you're trapped in a house with both of us."

Her eyes flashed. "You're being incredibly childish, you know that? And ignorant and *dumb*. I'm sorry for you."

"Yes, I suppose you are. I shouldn't really be nasty like this. I never said anything to you directly. I never put myself on the line. That's the politician in me. Hedging my bets. It backfired. My fault. You can take this as my concession speech."

She shook her head. "Why would you even *think* of hurting your career this way?"

The lines of his face turned bitter. "Because I don't get to meet too many real people, too many special people who are alive and giving and honest. You're worth being foolish over. But it *is* foolish, or course, so let's leave it at that."

She struggled to find something nice and reassuring to say. But there was nothing, Martin had embarrassed himself, and he wasn't wrong, just misguided. It surprised and moved her to know that she could have that effect on a man like Martin—on any guy, for that matter. It was another part of this strange summer of her life, when all the rules changed.

"I still want to campaign for you," she said. "Can I?"

He fingered the gun. "I wouldn't be without your help."

She sat back, a little drained. "Will you really use that?"

He laughed. "I hope not. I'd probably shoot my toe off. Ted thinks I'm a scream. He was a Green Beret in Vietnam. He's seen marines shoot pieces of themselves off even after training."

"Then maybe you should return the gun. I don't want you to wound yourself."

"I can't be a sitting duck. If this house is going to become an armed camp, I'm arming first."

She clenched her hands. "Armed camp. What a bad dream. There's got to be a way out of it."

"There is," Martin said. "But your great-uncle Gordon is making sure it's a bloody way."

She ate a light lunch, a small fruit salad, unable to summon a decent appetite. The day slogged on, the rain steady and unrelenting. She went upstairs, changed into her bathing suit, knotted a robe around her body, and went to the indoor pool, eager to swim and to work off some of the anxiety. To think.

Rain sheeted the glass wall, and the gray landscape beyond seemed to press the steamy room closer. Alison dove quickly into the pool and swam three laps before resting, throwing her head back to breathe the chlorinated air.

It didn't seem possible that the whole week would pass without a resolution. None of these guests would sit still for a week. She tried to hold on to that idea, and believe that it was more than a fragile hope. She breathed the hope into a prayer.

She ducked under the water and surfaced again, turned over to backstroke. She heard the door to the room open and close. She heard it being locked.

Her throat tightened. She righted herself in the water and saw Dana Mallory, rifle in hand. But the rifle looked different. There was a device attached to the barrel that made it longer, more ominous.

Mallory aimed the rifle at her. "There's a silencer on this gun," he said. His voice echoed against the tile and marble. "You know how much one of those babies costs? Plenty. But worth it. Always find use for it."

He approached the pool's edge. Alison found it difficult to breathe. Blood hammered in her ears. Mallory grinned smugly. As she watched, transfixed, he pulled the trigger.

Alison winced. There was a muffled thump and a sudden splash near her head. It took a few seconds for her to realize that a bullet had grazed her. That knowledge broke the spell. She gasped and tried to swim away. Mallory followed her, aimed, and squeezed off a second shot. The bullet skipped like a flat rock across the surface of the pool and caromed into the tiled side. Alison stopped, turned to face him.

"Now," he said. "You've heard of shooting fish in a barrel. I didn't like being interrupted when I was asking you questions. I don't think we'll be interrupted now."

"You won't shoot me," she said, trying to make her voice even. "It would be stupid."

He kept the rifle trained on her. "You don't know what I'll do. That's why you'll talk to me."

"You heard what Uncle Gordon said . . ."

The third shot nearly sliced her throat. She cried out, flattening against the side of the pool. Mallory's expression had changed to anger.

"I want answers," he said. "I want to know why Andrew Fallon is here and why Martin Young is here. I want to know what Gordon Foxworth really has in mind. You know it all, sister. You're not here for a good time. He's your relative. Now I'm telling you, I am a desperate man and I will hurt you if I have to. We'll stay here all day if you want that."

Alison trembled in the water. "I don't know anything," she said.

Mallory clicked the safety on the rifle. "Let's try again."

Anger began to crowd the terror out of Alison. She was sick and tired of being bullied. The frustration of being helpless only fueled the slow fury. She looked at Mallory, and he represented Uncle Gordon and this estate, and this situation.

She had an idea, a stupid, suicidal idea, but she allowed herself to plan it out. It all depended on Mallory—if he was really crazy enough to kill her. She'd faced guns before, and cruel men, but she'd always had some landscape to use in a getaway.

"Let's go," Mallory snapped. "Or would you like to see how fast you can do laps?"

He raised the rifle again. She wrapped her arms across her chest, feeling physically ill. She gasped when fists pounded on the door outside.

Mallory swore. He kept the rifle aimed at her. "Keep quiet," he hissed.

"Mallory!" the voice was familiar. Not Jeff, or Martin, or Uncle Gordon.

Mallory's eyes twitched. The pounding came again. "Mallory, open this door. If you've hurt her . . ."

Now there was silence and a sudden crash. Whoever was out there was breaking down the door. Mallory breathed rapidly. "If anyone breaks in here, you're a bloody little girl. You'd better stop him right now."

Alison could barely think. "Please," she called out. "Don't come in. I'm alone in here."

Silence. "Are you sure?" the voice insisted.

Mallory moved to the edge of the pool. "Tell the man you're sure."

Alison struggled in an agony of indecision. Like standing at the edge of an icy lake, trying to build courage to plunge in. Only the first seconds hurt, and the worst was the anticipation . . .

"Miss Thorne, are you really alone?"

"Come on!" Mallory snarled. "Tell him."

Alison filled her lungs and ducked under the water. The coolness closed over her, shutting out noise. She opened her eyes to the blue-green world, and stroked as hard as she could. Her shoulders and back trembled in expectation of the ripping bullet. When the first bullet came, it sheared the water a yard from her side, clouding the pool. The second bullet sliced in front of her. She wriggled to move faster, saw Mallory's shoe tip.

She surfaced with a raking gasp of air and wrapped her hands around Mallory's legs. She yanked with desperate strength and the surprised Mallory toppled, the rifle flying. He hit the surface of the water with a sickening smack and flailed, his clothes ballooning. Alison gripped the edge of the pool.

"Mallory's here!" she screamed. "Hurry!"

Her last word was cut off by Mallory's hand over her mouth. She struggled to hang on to the side of the pool, but Mallory was as strong as he looked. She was dragged away and an arm tightened around her, pinning her arms. She couldn't move her head. Mallory's breath rasped in her ear.

Then she was underwater, the pool rushing into her nose. She opened her eyes wide with terror, Mallory's hand blocking air. The pressure in her lungs was intolerable. She writhed against his power, helpless.

Through the gathering blackness, she heard a crash, magnified and drawn out by the water. She heard clattering footsteps and she heard the thundering crash of a gun. The crash spread and rippled and was the last thing she heard before she blacked out.

9 • Visit to the Doctor

She retained enough consciousness to know that she was in the pool, and that she had to have air. She flailed, horrified to find her arms useless. Her face broke the surface. The air was thick like molasses, and she clawed at it, afraid for her life.

She heard a voice laced with panic. The possibility of drowning was very real. Her hand hit something slippery and hard: the edge of the pool. She closed her fingers over it and groped with her other hand. Hanging on, she pulled herself against the wall of the pool and rested her forehead against the tile. She waited until her breath stopped rasping in her throat, until her eyes began to clear.

Her arms burned with effort and she tried to call out for help. A croak issued from her mouth, hardly intelligible. But she could see now, and she saw Dr. Preston, standing over her. He held a revolver in his hand. He looked helpless and frightened.

She threw back her head, baring her teeth. A clattering came from outside the room. Then voices. Shapes materialized over her, familiar shapes, not recognizable because she was slipping back into semi-consciousness. But now a strong hand seized her arms and, with a sob, she let go and gave herself to the strength of her rescuers. The hands pulled her from the water and she lay on her back. Lips touched hers and for a moment she thought someone was kissing her. Her eyes opened, and saw Jeff's face, white and tense. She realized that he was giving her artificial respiration. It struck her as funny and she laughed, but the laugh became a fit of coughing.

She raked air through a pinhole in her throat, but slowly the pinhole widened and soon she was breathing steadily, if not normally.

"I feel silly," she whispered.

Jeff was trembling slightly. "You'll be okay now."

She turned her head, saw Ed Ginger standing near Dr. Preston. "Thanks," she said.

Ed nodded, with a brief smile. He turned to Jeff. "I'd better go look for Mallory."

Jeff nodded, still kneeling next to Alison. Ed Ginger left. She shivered. "Where is Mallory now?"

"We don't know," Jeff said. "He ran past us, soaking wet. Did he try to drown you?"

Alison struggled to sit up, and Jeff helped her, supporting her. "Only as a last resort," she said.

Jeff looked grim. "He carried a rifle."

"Yes. With a silencer."

Jeff's voice was thin. "Did he try to kill you?"

"No. He tried to scare me. He wanted answers again. But I didn't know the answers."

"What kind of answers?"

Dr. Preston cleared his throat. He seemed shaken by these events. "Excuse me," he said. "I wasn't much help at saving her from the pool, but I *am* a doctor. I think it would be wise to get her into warm clothes and give her something hot to drink, instead of questioning her right here."

Jeff looked at her long and hard. "Okay. Give me a hand."

Dr. Preston reached down and helped Jeff lift Alison to her feet. Dizziness swept over her, but she battled it and was able to walk, with Jeff and Dr. Preston supporting her.

Ed Ginger provided hot tea and honey in a recipe he claimed was his own. Alison sat warmly in a stuffed chair, staring at the sheep's head over the fireplace, sipping the sweet concoction. It tasted weird, but warmth flowed through her body and relaxed her. She'd bundled into a sweater and jeans and socks and dried her hair with a towel. It hung rather limply now, but she'd been in no shape to use the blow dryer.

Jeff sat near her. He watched her closely, and she smiled when she noticed him.

"You look worried," she said.

"Yeah, I'm worried. I'm scared to death."

She sipped the drink. "So am I."

"Does Uncle Gordon know?"

Alison shrugged. "He must know by now."

"Well, if Preston doesn't tell him, I will. If I can find him. This has gone too far."

"I agree."

Jeff was trying very hard to be courageous for her sake, but his fear showed. She liked him for that.

"What happened, anyway?" he asked.

She told him briefly, unemotionally. "I don't know why Dr. Preston saved me," she said. "I thought he was in with the other two."

"Maybe he was," Jeff said. "But Mallory might be a little too much for the others."

"But what are they trying to find out? He keeps asking me

what Martin is doing here, and what Fallon is doing here. But I don't know. I don't even know what *Mallory* is doing here."

Jeff sighed. "I think it's becoming fairly obvious."

"How?"

"I think Mallory took that potshot at Uncle Gordon. And I think *he* thinks that Uncle Gordon knows. And Mallory is running scared."

Alison cupped the drink in her hands. A laziness suffused her limbs, a need to sleep. "Why would Mallory shoot Uncle Gordon?"

"Why not? I think if we knew the details, we'd trace it to this big deal they're cooking up. Mallory is in trouble with the mob. He must need money in a hurry. He may have made this deal with Uncle Gordon and then Uncle Gordon changed his mind."

"But killing Uncle Gordon—how would it help?"

Jeff turned his eyes to the window and watched the endless rain trickle down the glass. "I don't know. Unless it had to do with Uncle Gordon's will."

Alison brooded over the drink. "His will again. My father mentioned Uncle Gordon's will. He thought I might be a big beneficiary. He thought that's why Uncle Gordon asked me here."

Jeff looked at her. "Is it a possibility?"

"I don't know. I doubt it. Anyway, my father never guessed any of this would happen. Neither did Gramps. He thought it might be some important scoop about Mr. Fallon, but I *know* he didn't suspect what Uncle Gordon is doing."

Jeff smiled. "You sound very close to your dad and grandpa."

It hurt to think about it. "Very close. And with my brother Eric. We fight like most families, and we have our differences, but we like each other. I'll tell you one thing. I wish

I were back there now. What about you?"

Jeff stood, a hand on the mantel. "My folks separated when I was about ten. I was brought up by my mother and by various uncles when my mother went on her jaunts. She lives in California now, and my father is in South Africa on business. I have two sisters out west somewhere, with families, but they don't write much. I've been on my own since I was fifteen."

"What brought you to Long Island?"

"I grew up here. My mother moved to California about a year ago, but my father still has a condominium in Smithtown."

He smiled sheepishly and sat again. He hadn't intended to talk about himself.

"I kind of envy you," Alison said moodily. "You're making it on your own. I feel like a parasite."

A gust of wind drove the rain against the windows. "I'd give my right arm for a family," Jeff said. He laughed. "Right now, I'd give my right arm to get out of this place."

"Where's your journalistic spirit?" Alison chided. "You have a dramatic story here."

"Sure. Millionaire goes bats on Long Island. Alison, listen. Don't go off alone anymore. Always be with somebody—me, Ed, even Martin Young. Anywhere so that Mallory can't get at you."

She watched him, knowing that he was sincere, knowing that his words were well meant. But a sense of anger rippled through her again, the odd sensation that this was all a setup, a hoax. But what kind of hoax included a desperate man with a rifle? A man who tried to drown her?

She turned her head and watched the rivulets of rain on the windows. It was nice sitting here with Jeff, sipping this vile drink. There was a pleasant relaxation to it. She didn't care to pursue demons any further now.

But Alison disobeyed Jeff almost immediately. Later in the day, after a light snack, she saw Dr. Preston head for the library, with Cory Shaw following closely. She waited a few moments, then followed them, pausing a few steps from the library door. She could hear voices inside: Preston's, Shaw's, and Mallory's. The words were muffled and she pressed her ear to the wall.

She heard Dr. Preston's voice first. "No!" Preston was shouting. "It's gone far enough!"

"I ought to shoot you," Mallory snarled.

"It was a fool stunt," Cory Shaw put in. "A fool stunt."

"You agreed to let me handle it," Mallory said. "It's got to work sooner or later."

"But she might die before then," Preston argued. "Listen, man, she nearly drowned today."

"Before you shot at me," Mallory said.

"It's a good thing I brought my pistol," Preston said. "You're tough, Dana, but you're stupid."

There was a scuffling of chairs and a thud. Then Mallory's voice, ragged. "I don't want to hear that again."

There was coughing, and then Shaw's voice. "Keep it down, will you? We'll have the whole house outside the room."

The voices continued, but lowered, so that Alison could not make out the words. She heard Fallon's name mentioned, and Martin's, and Uncle Gordon's. But it made no sense. She began to be frightened of discovery.

The voices stopped abruptly and she backed away from the door. She heard a man's breath behind her and used all of her willpower to avoid screaming.

She turned, and faced Murdoch.

"Should I tell 'em you're out here?" Murdoch said.

She stared into the wizened face, thinking furiously. "I just happened by," she said. "I wanted to do some reading."

"Ye wanted to eavesdrop," Murdoch said. "I've a mind to drag ye into the room by the scruff of your neck and let ye take your punishment."

Anger flooded her. "Why?" she demanded. "What have I done to offend you?"

Murdoch's lip trembled. "I've been with Mr. Foxworth for thirty-five years. I joined him in his sorrow. It was our place, until you came, and brought this trouble."

His anguish was real. "I didn't bring the trouble," she said. "Uncle Gordon invited me here for ten days. I thought it would be a vacation. I didn't invite these other people, or imprison them. Ask your employer about that."

Murdoch closed one eye and regarded her wickedly. "You're the cause of it. Mr. Foxworth dotes on you, and he's forgotten everything else."

"I don't think he dotes on me very much, Murdoch. I was nearly drowned today and he hasn't come forward to see if I'm alive."

Murdoch seemed surprised at her words. He shrugged and turned, retreating down the corridor. Alison watched him go, chilled by the frost of his hatred. She didn't blame him for hating her. Murdoch would hate anybody who diverted Uncle Gordon's attention. Foxworth Hall was Uncle Gordon's world. Uncle Gordon was Murdoch's world. She stopped suspecting Murdoch, as she'd done, in the back of her mind. Murdoch was not guilty. He was only broken.

She heard the library door open, and whirled as Mallory and Shaw emerged. They looked at her oddly.

"How long have you been out here?" Mallory demanded.

"For a while," she said, tasting her fear. "I was talking with Murdoch."

"Talking or listening?" Mallory asked.

Shaw placed a restraining arm on Mallory's shoulder. "Come on, Dana. Not now."

Mallory shrugged off the arm and raked Alison with his eyes for a long moment. Alison forced herself to stay with those eyes, but she could see nothing. There was more to Dana Mallory than his brutality. He'd nearly drowned her this morning, but he looked at her with curiosity. He finally turned from her and went with Cory Shaw down the corridor. Alison felt slightly weak when he'd gone.

She looked at the library door, slightly ajar. Dr. Preston remained inside. She'd done no investigating so far, though the intention had crossed her mind. She'd been too busy dodging disaster. Now she had the opportunity.

Nervous, she gripped the doorknob and entered the library. A low lamp burned and cast a warm glow on the book cases, and on the impressive form of Dr. Preston. He sat smoking a pipe, staring into the fireplace.

"How much did you hear?" he asked.

She reflected ruefully that she was a terrible detective. "Not much," she said.

Dr. Preston turned to her. A livid bruise had begun to swell beneath his left eye. Alison caught her breath.

"Did you hear Mallory give me this?"

"I heard you fighting. I didn't know he hit you."

Dr. Preston clamped his teeth around the pipe. "If you're going to sit down, then do it. You make me nervous standing there."

Alison sat on the sofa, tense. She ran her tongue over dry lips. "I wanted to thank you for saving me today."

Preston grunted. "I thought I saw Mallory head for the pool but I wasn't sure. Then your boyfriend told me you'd gone swimming and I knew Mallory was in there with you. Mallory and his silencer."

Preston sounded disgusted. Alison wondered who he meant by her boyfriend. She'd mentioned to both Martin and Jeff that she felt like taking a swim.

"Why do you hang around with him?" she asked.

"We're business partners," he said. "Mallory, Cory Shaw, your great-uncle, and myself. We met through business deals, and we've stayed together through business deals. Cory Shaw has been a golfing partner, which makes it a social thing. But not Mallory. He doesn't play golf with anybody. And Gordon Foxworth doesn't leave his estate."

"Except to get shot at."

Preston looked narrowly at her. "That's right. I didn't do it, you know."

"I didn't know. Do you think I'm the jury also?"

Preston raised an eyebrow.

"Andrew Fallon thinks Uncle Gordon called me here to finger the guilty party."

Preston guffawed. "Fallon is a bloody fool. A failure as a man and a disaster as a politician."

Alison smiled. "Martin would be glad to know you feel that way."

"Martin is going to lose the election," Preston said.

"I think he has a good chance."

"He has looks and charisma," Preston said. "But Fallon has more money for media saturation, and he has the right opinions."

"I'm confused. It's hard to know whom you're backing."

Preston leaned back, dwarfing the love seat. "I'm backing Fallon, of course. Martin Young is against monopolies and trusts and private ownership of land. How do you think millionaires make their money?"

"I don't know, Dr. Preston. I haven't known many millionaires."

Preston looked at the books, studying the bindings. "I do think you're here for a reason. Not to choose the man who shot at Foxworth. I'm not an idiot, like Fallon. But you're the key."

"*I'm* the idiot," she said hotly. "For staying here."

Preston regarded her lazily. "You're really a lucky little girl, you know. Your grandfather is Vice President. Your great-uncle is Gordon Foxworth. So a snip like you can waltz into this library and chat with me."

She swallowed a surge of anger. "Well, you may be a snob, but you're honest."

"Of course I'm a snob," Preston said. "I was born into wealth. I went to medical school as a lark. I was always a lousy doctor. But I had influence. Doors opened magically. I rose swiftly to a lucrative practice among rich female hypochondriacs dripping with excess flesh and money. I became the executive director of Westwood General, and I sit on prestigious medical boards. All very neat. I stepped on people like you. I shouldn't even agree to be in the same room with you."

Preston laughed again, winced, and touched his bruise. "You're a cute kid, Miss Thorne. Perhaps I'll let you into Westwood, even without money. On the basis of wit alone—and political connections. I can toady with the best of them. Of course, I won't have much to say about it after this week. No doubt Caryl Mason has sealed up my office."

"Who's Caryl Mason?" she asked. "You mentioned him before."

Preston sucked on his pipe. "Caryl Mason is on the board of Westwood General. A civilian. He has delusions about running a top-notch hospital. He harbors odd ideas about having a superb doctor as Executive Director. He dared to call me an incompetent fool, a disgrace to medicine, a charlatan hiding behind my family's millions. He lucked out when I was implicated in several scandals—salesmen operating on patients, misappropriation of funds—all blown up in the newspapers. Mason suggested I leave, and he started proceedings to force me out. Does it make your blood boil?"

Alison studied him. "Is it true?"

Preston took the pipe from his mouth, held it reflectively. "Of course it's true, every word of it. Caryl Mason came along at the right time. My entire family is in trouble. The Prestons have been caught in several stock swindles, a real estate scandal, dirty dealings with foreign cartels. We are a stain on the escutcheon of the North Shore. We're an embarrassment, calling repugnant attention to the best families. We're dangerous. After all, if the Prestons can sin, what about the other leading clans? The Prestons must be swept under the rug, and quickly.

"And Caryl Mason is the man to do it. Distinguished yet sexy, of good blood and breeding, but not *too* rich. Others can feel superior to him, yet depend on him. A good administrator, that's what Caryl is. They love him. And he gets to them. Look at the great medical centers, he cries. Westwood languished because Westwood has no great doctor. Westwood only has Jonas Preston. Scion of a scummy family. Lousy sawbones. Now Mason just happens to know Dr. Eliot Foreman, the transplant surgeon now practicing in Atlanta. Making all the news magazines, the late night talk shows. Mason can get him. Once Preston is out."

Preston stuck the pipe back in his mouth. The pungent smoke wreathed the library. Alison found herself fascinated.

"That's what's happening now," he continued. "My execution. And once I'm out, what then? My own hospital, of course. Among the less sterling, among the silver plate people, I would have a lush following. The comfortable middle class, the *nouveau riche*. They would come, glad to get me, because my reputation is unstained. The financial flummery is a darkly kept secret among the upper crust. But to start a hospital, I need capital and real estate. Land, Miss Thorne. Land such as Foxworth Hall. And if Gordon Foxworth were dead, perhaps I could claim this land. Perhaps there are contracts, deals, naming me as owner. If Foxworth dies. Enough reason to take a shot at him, right Miss Thorne?"

Alison moistened her mouth. "But you're lying."

Preston smiled. "Of course I'm lying. There are no such deals. There is no motive. And if there is no motive, Miss Thorne, why am I here?"

"And Shaw and Mallory," Alison added.

Preston puffed. "They may have motives," he said. "You ought to ask them."

"Mallory tried to kill me."

Preston leaned forward, eyes gleaming. "That's right. Then perhaps you should ask your great-uncle why he's here. And why I'm here."

Alison sensed that Preston was circling a point. "He won't tell me," she said.

Preston was leaning so close to her now that his breath became sour in her nose. "He'd best tell you. It might mean your life."

Alison's heart pounded. "Is that a threat, Dr. Preston?"

"That, my dear girl, is a friendly warning. I did not receive this black eye from a rational man. My fate is intertwined with Mallory's. Our fate with Gordon Foxworth's. And with you. Do you begin to understand?"

"I'm not sure."

"Be sure. I can't say that I like you. I probably don't. But I wouldn't enjoy seeing you killed."

He roused himself from the love seat and exited from the library, the thin whirl of pipe smoke lingering behind him, acrid and ominous. Alison sat quietly on the sofa, trying to make sense of his story, of his words. But she felt no closer to an answer than before.

The pipe smoke dissipated, leaving a bitter flavor in the room. Alison began to feel cold, as if something dreadful were happening outside the house, some shambling monster stalking the fogged meadow, snuffling at the walls, at the wall where she sat. She was terribly frightened, an intuitive fear.

She was not surprised to hear running feet. She could taste the disaster.

Murdoch came hurtling into the room, and Alison sprang from the sofa, for a moment thinking that he was attacking her. But he slumped against a bookcase and raked air between chattering teeth. Ed Ginger appeared behind him, flushed. Alison realized that Ed had pushed Murdoch into the room.

Ed stared around the library, let his eyes light on Alison. "Have you been with Jeff Harmon?"

Alison's throat tightened. "No. What's wrong?"

Murdoch coughed bitterly. Ed struggled to catch his breath. "Jeff had some coffee with me before. He said he was going to take some pictures in the rain. For atmosphere. I thought maybe he hadn't gone out yet."

Alison glanced at Murdoch. "Why shouldn't he go out?"

Ed glared at the white-faced servant. "Tell her, Murdoch."

Murdoch's eyes rolled in fear. His lower lip trembled as he stared at Alison. "It's my job," he stammered. "I do it all the time for Mr. Foxworth. I've done it for years. I see no reason to stop now. I thought everyone was inside."

Alison swayed slightly. "What did you do?"

Ed rested against the doorpost. "He let the dogs loose."

The vision flashed across her mind swiftly and vividly. Jeff at the perimeter of the woods. The rush of the dogs, the spring for the throat, the teeth sinking into his flesh.

Alison sideswiped Ed Ginger as she ran from the library, and she had to steady herself against the wall as she moved through the corridor. She took a wrong turn, retraced her steps, and found the foyer.

She saw Fallon and his wife, Jill and Ted, and Dr. Preston. Ignoring them, she tore aside the curtain on the bay window

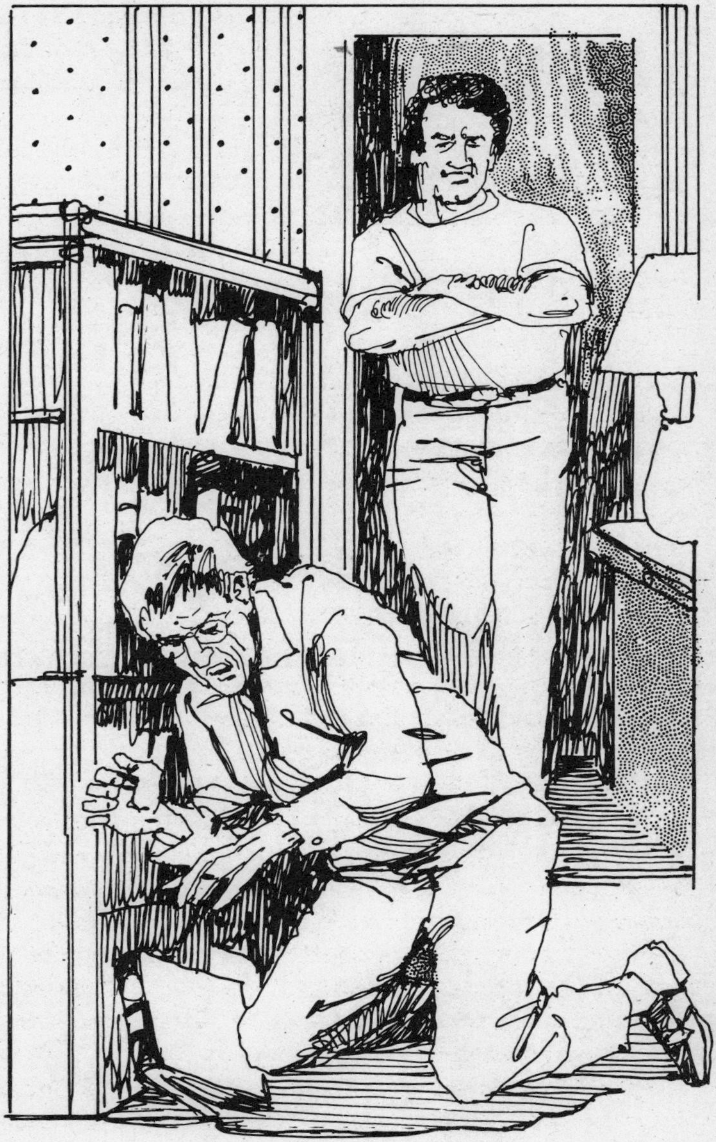

and looked out, past the rivers of rain, to the darkening grass and the blue haze of the woods. She saw Jeff as he emerged from the forest, camera slung over his shoulder. He walked slowly.

She stood frozen for a moment, then forced herself to leave the window, to run to the door. She unlatched the door, pulled it open. The rain hissed in the soaked, fragrant air. She saw nothing but Jeff, trudging slowly toward the house.

"Jeff!" she shouted. He looked up, waved.

"Jeff, run! The dogs are loose!"

She saw the gray, matted streak before Jeff did. The shepherd was joined by another, and a third. As a pack, as wolves in the gathering night, they hurtled across the beautiful landscape. Jeff turned, and his eyes showed disbelief. He pumped strength into his legs and broke into a desperate run, but the dogs were at his heels. In seconds, they would bring him down.

Alison was outside in the rain, running toward him, stupidly, helplessly. The first shot brought her to a terrified stop. The lead dog was hurled backward, as if he'd run into a stone wall. Two more cracks echoed in the closing night. The remaining dogs writhed in midstride, fell. The sudden stillness on the heels of their charge made Alison draw a sharp breath.

She saw Jeff stop, look behind, bewildered. Then she saw the figure emerging from the woods, and turned her attention to him. It was Martin. His rifle was still smoking.

10 • Clue in the Cabin

Alison blinked back the rain in her eyes and went to Jeff. She shivered once as she realized how vulnerable she'd made herself.

"Are you okay?" she asked.

Jeff nodded, dazed. "They came out of nowhere. How did they get loose?"

"Murdoch turned them loose. He claims he always does it, to exercise them."

"Not with a houseful of company," Jeff said with asperity.

Martin trotted up to them, his hair tousled. "That was close," he said.

Jeff smiled weakly. "I sort of owe you my life."

"Sort of," Martin said bleakly. "I'm glad I was within target range."

"I'm glad you decided to walk around in the rain too," Jeff amended.

I was in my room," Martin said. "I heard footsteps outside the door. When I opened the door, someone disappeared around the corner. I grabbed the rifle and followed. I got to the back door in time to see a figure running toward the woods. I ran after him. It was dumb, but I was sore. I lost him in the woods, and I was just returning."

Martin shouldered the gun. "Well, I don't know about you, but I intend to get in out of the rain." He started for the house.

"Martin?" said Jeff, and Martin turned. "Did you see who it was?"

"Who?" Martin asked.

"The guy you chased."

"No. I never got a good look. He wore a raincoat—a tan raincoat. Maybe his, maybe not. That's all I saw."

He turned and continued on, jogging. Jeff stood in the rain and watched him. "Lousy chaser," he said.

"Come on," Alison urged. "Let's go inside."

Jeff set his jaw. "Yes. I want to talk to Murdoch."

She walked back with him and found an excited crowd in the foyer. Eyes followed them as they came in and closed the door. Andrew Fallon was on his feet, hands clenched at his sides.

"I'd say that was a murder attempt," he said.

Jeff looked at him. "Why me, Fallon?"

Fallon stared around, as if seeking help. "I don't know. Maybe *you* have an explanation."

Fallon's eyes were bloodshot. His face was lined. He was under tremendous strain. Laura Fallon seemed to sink into herself, white and shaking.

"I don't have an explanation," Jeff said coldly. "I didn't shoot at Gordon Foxworth, if that's what you mean."

"You have a motive," Fallon said.

Jeff placed his hands on his hips. "What motive?"

Fallon licked his lips. He was a marked contrast to Jeff. Jeff stood firmly, soaked by the rain, youthful and angry. Fallon trembled as he accused; a tired old lion.

"You were doing a story on Westwood, on that area," he said. "You were planning a story on Foxworth. Foxworth is pals with Dr. Preston, and those other two. Maybe the story was an exposé. Maybe Foxworth didn't want it printed and put pressure on your editor. Maybe you figured with Foxworth out of the way, you could make a name for yourself."

"That's insane."

Fallon cocked his head to one side, a nervous tic. "Maybe it's insane, maybe not. The fact is, *you* were singled out."

"So was Martin Young," Jeff said. "What's *his* motive?"

Fallon retreated. "I don't know. I don't know why *I'm* here."

Jill laughed lightly. "None of us knows why he's here," she said.

Alison looked at her. Jill and Ted blended into the background here. Of all the guests, they acted less like prisoners than the others. But then, Martin was the prisoner, and they were his adjuncts, his pilot fish. They were not intended to express emotion, only to exist. But they existed glamorously. Jill, in a clinging white dress of Indian design, looked sylphlike and ethereal. Ted smoked a cigarette crookedly; a bored man.

Alison's attention was wrested by the appearance, sudden and silent, of Uncle Gordon and Murdoch. Murdoch almost cringed, a twisted Rigoletto to Uncle Gordon's Duke. Jeff's chest heaved with angry breath as he turned to face Uncle Gordon.

"What happened?" Uncle Gordon asked.

"Let's skip the garbage," Jeff said. "You know what happened. Your servant let the dogs loose. While I was outside."

"I didn't know ye were out there," Murdoch whined.

"He knew. He probably knew Martin Young was out there, also. Luckily, he didn't know that Young is a crack shot."

144

Foxworth turned to Martin, who stood uneasily in a corner. "I didn't know that either."

"Don't change the subject," Jeff snapped. "I think time is up for your game. Nobody's confessing to anything and we've got a growing casualty list. Young, Alison, now me. We're trapped in this haunted house with a nut, and a servant who gets rid of unwanted guests by killing them. I don't think we'll *last* a week."

Uncle Gordon smiled shallowly. "It's Tuesday night. Only a few days to go."

Jeff's body tensed with fury. "I said we want out."

Fallon rose to add his voice, but he was crushed by Foxworth, who spoke swiftly and with acid in his voice.

"You're not getting out," Foxworth said. "Not you, or anybody, until the end of the week. Until I find out the truth. I know that you're turning on each other. I expected that. It's a pitiful spectacle. It may get worse, until you all wring confessions out of each other. That's your problem."

He looked around, saw that the group was cowed. "You can sue me when you leave, or try to have me arrested. Whatever you like. For this week, you're stuck. Make the best of it.

"As for Mr. Murdoch. He has been with me for half a lifetime. We grew old together. He was always a bit dour and eager to protect my privacy. It was a good relationship. But I see that age and fear have twisted his loyalties. He failed to tell Alison of the dogs when she arrived here. She might have been killed. Now he's nearly caused the death of another guest. I think it will stand as proof of my honest intentions that I'm now asking Mr. Murdoch to leave my employment."

Murdoch turned to gape at Foxworth, his face a mask of terror. His hands moved unwittingly into a gesture of supplication.

"Things change," Foxworth said. He spoke to Murdoch,

though his eyes, sad and haunted, remained fixed ahead. "The world changes. Foxworth Hall is not what it was. Nor am I. Nor any of us. We do not live in a comic opera world any more. I'm sorry, Murdoch. I'll give you excellent reference. You will leave in the morning."

Murdoch turned away his aged body rigid with grief. Alison ached for him.

Foxworth's lips made a thin bitter line as he surveyed his puzzled audience. "You see? I've made a sacrifice. I've chopped off a part of my life. I am not playing games, Mr. Harmon. I am out to discover truth. The discovery will hurt me as much as it will hurt the offender. I'm in this to the end. Now you know how serious I am."

He turned abruptly and left the foyer. Murdoch stayed for only a moment, then followed him. Alison went to the doorway, stepped into the empty corridor. Jeff was abruptly behind her.

"I don't understand it," he said softly.

"I do," she said. "I think I do. Some of it anyway. He's telling the truth, Jeff. It isn't a game. And he's after more than a man who took a potshot at him."

"All right, what is he after?"

Alison smiled. "The truth."

"That's good. I hope he finds it."

She faced Jeff, terribly aware of the dark turn things had taken. "I'm finding out a lot of things myself."

"Like what?"

"Martin Young was pretty serious about me. I didn't know that. And Uncle Gordon has feelings. And Dr. Preston has problems. I've been pretty busy running around the world trying to do everything, and I guess I missed a lot."

"Well, I guess you learn as you get older."

"We may not have time," she whispered. "We've got to figure out these people in a couple of days."

Jeff let out a slow, nervous breath and said, "I hope we have terrific intuition."

Clouds skittered across a turgid sky early the next morning, but by nine o'clock, pallid sunlight appeared. Alison awoke and, following an instinct, looked out her bedroom window. She saw the stooped figure of Murdoch, dressed in an old suit, wispy hair awry in the wind. He carried two battered suitcases and William stood stiffly by the Lincoln. Uncle Gordon strode to Murdoch, shook his hand solemnly. Murdoch pushed the suitcases into the back seat of the Lincoln, and followed them. Uncle Gordon shut the door.

William took the driver's seat—Alison noted a smirk on his face—and the Lincoln drove away. Uncle Gordon stood for a long time and watched, but she couldn't see his face from this angle. She tried to imagine the emotional impact on Uncle Gordon of giving up this piece of his life. Powerful, she assumed. And he was doing it because Murdoch could not cope with the present, with reality. Which meant that Uncle Gordon, at last, could cope.

Then why was he holding everyone prisoner and behaving like a paranoid fool?

She mulled the questions, trying to find an answer. She imagined Eric, sailing in the Caribbean, and she sighed. She had very little time to find the answers.

The forest shivered with sudden winds and the glitter of sunlight. The earth was dank and loamy, rich with rainy fragrance. Alison followed Jeff, who poked his way among the trees, keeping to the path and stopping now and then.

"What are you looking for?" Alison asked. She couldn't keep a note of annoyance from her voice.

Jeff looked sweaty and disturbed himself. "I'm not sure," he said curtly. "Just bear with me."

"I'll bear with you, but give me a clue. We've been tromping through the woods for an hour now."

"Twenty-five minutes." Jeff chewed his lip, and his face showed a struggle with his ego. "Okay," he said. "I was hoping to put together a convincing case, but it doesn't look like anything else was left behind. When I went out yesterday, I didn't go to take pictures. I'd come across something the other day that interested me, and I wanted to be pretty sure of being in the woods alone."

"It wasn't a brilliant move," Alison said. She wiped her forehead with the back of her hand.

Jeff smiled. "True. Anyway, what I found was in the hunters' cabin. Come on, I'll show you."

They hurried along the path. At one point she stopped, and Jeff turned to her.

"What's up?"

She shook her head. "Nothing. I thought I heard someone following us."

Jeff peered into the trees. "I don't see anything."

"Well, if we stopped, whoever is following us would probably hide."

Jeff stepped off the path, plunged a few yards into the woods. "I still don't see anything."

Alison became impatient. "Well, I probably imagined it."

"No, if someone's following us, I want to know."

"Jeff, it's okay. You wouldn't find anything."

Jeff turned, eyeing her. "You're pretty jittery."

"I want to see what you found."

"But if somebody's following us, don't you want to find out who it is?"

"No."

Jeff put his hands on his hips, blew out a tired breath. "Okay. Forget it."

He moved on. Alison walked behind him, upset. She never

shied away from danger, but Mallory had rattled her, and she knew it.

The hunters' cabin appeared in its clearing, pristine and slightly menacing. They approached it with some trepidation and Alison would not have been surprised to see Mallory spring from the door, gun blazing.

They reached the door without mishap, however, and Jeff closed his hand on the knob.

"Should we knock?" Alison asked.

"No." Jeff pushed open the door.

There was a flurry of movement in the cabin. A crash of glass and a thud of somebody pushing over a chair. Alison seized Jeff's arm.

"Who's there?" Jeff yelled, in an unsteady voice.

A scraping noise told that the cabin's visitor had left via the window. Jeff and Alison moved into the coolness of the cabin. Jeff closed the door behind them.

They searched the few rooms, but whoever escaped was apparently the only inhabitant. Jeff scooped up a chewed cigar butt.

"Mallory's," he said.

"Well," Alison said, looking at the butt. "We might have figured that Mallory would come here during his hunts."

"But why would he run out?"

"If it was Mallory," Alison pointed out.

Jeff dropped the butt. "Okay. If it was Mallory."

Alison shrugged. "I don't know."

Jeff sat on a wooden chair and drummed on the table. "I can't crack this thing."

"Nobody said you had to."

Jeff made a face. "I like to think of myself as a pretty good reporter. Powers of observation. Deduction. Maybe I watch too much television. But I've always been good at figuring things. I psyche out whodunits before the first commercial."

Alison said, "Remind me never to watch a mystery with you."

He managed a smile. "I keep my mouth shut. Anyway, this has me going. And if I could dope it out, I'd have a story for *The Islander.*"

Alison sat on the other wooden chair. "What did you find here?"

Jeff got up from his chair and went to the sofa that dominated one wall. "I put it back," he said. "I found it here, behind the couch."

Alison followed him and watched as he grasped the back of the sofa and bent down. His fingers grappled for something. "I thought it was a handkerchief or something, but it wasn't," he said. "I almost broke my neck pulling it out."

"Let's see."

He straightened up, his hand trailing a long black length of cloth. He held it up to Alison, like an angler displaying a fish. "Mean anything to you?"

She squinted at it. "No."

He smiled. "Took me quite a while to figure it out. But fortunately, I had seen one of them just recently, when I was covering an oil exporters' conference in Manhattan."

"I still don't get it," she said.

He draped the black cloth over both palms as if it were part of a minister's vestments. "Imagine it wrapped around a headdress and hanging down over the shoulder."

"*Headdress?*"

"Not Indian."

"Jeff, I don't like playing—" And then she realized. "*Oil* exporters—you mean an *Arab* headdress!"

"Bingo."

She reached out and took the cloth, let it slide through her fingers, feeling its rough texture. "The *ghutra* and *igal*," she said. "Of course. There was an Arab staying here?"

"Apparently," Jeff said.

"Why?"

Jeff's eyes were dark. "Business?"

"Business?" She gave the cloth back to Jeff and felt an ominous suffocation in the room. "Well, I guess Uncle Gordon would have business dealings with people from all over the world. What do *you* think?"

"I think Arabs have been buying a lot of United States real estate. Arabs and Frenchmen and other members of foreign cartels."

Alison's eyes grew bright with understanding. "You think Uncle Gordon is involved in that? What land does he have?"

"An awful lot of Long Island," Jeff said.

"And these men? Shaw, and Mallory, and Preston?"

"All here for a big business deal."

There was a heavy silence in the cabin, a feeling of anticipation. "Then we have to find out what the deal was, and why it has everybody at each other's throats."

"And ours," Jeff said.

She nodded, feeling cold. "Yes," she said. "And ours."

11 • Pilot Fish

Wednesday passed in bursts of sunshine, contrasted with lowering clouds. Mallory stayed out of sight. At four in the afternoon, Alison found herself in the foyer, alone. She curled up on a sofa with a paperback mystery she'd brought and tried to concentrate. It wasn't easy. Too many thoughts and questions filled her mind.

Incredibly, the week was passing. Tomorrow was Thursday. She wondered what would happen on the weekend. Whether Uncle Gordon would accuse anybody, and what he would do then. Or whether the nightmare would be over. She couldn't believe now that Uncle Gordon would give up and let them go. It had to end in violence. Maybe in death.

She wondered if the visit by an Arab businessman had anything to do with this week. If Uncle Gordon had brought Mallory, Preston and Shaw in on a big real estate deal, and one of them had gotten greedy—that would explain why Uncle Gordon was shot at. *If* he was shot at. If a huge deal was in the balance, it would explain why Uncle Gordon needed to unmask the traitor before contracts were signed.

Before money changed hands. But neither Mallory nor Dr. Preston had referred to any such deal, except obliquely.

And why was Martin here? And Jeff Harmon?

And Alison Thorne?

Cory Shaw wandered downstairs, alone. She watched him as he found a seat near her and picked up a hunting magazine. He wore a tasteless sport shirt and slacks, his gaunt body unable to support the clothing. His eyes flickered and briefly caught hers. She looked away.

"Stay out of the woods," he said.

The words came suddenly, and the flat voice startled her. She lowered the book and looked at him. "What?"

"You went into the woods today," he said. "Stay out."

She studied his dark, deepset eyes. "Did you follow us?"

"No. I just saw you go in. Mallory does a lot of hunting."

"And there might be a lucky accident."

"I'll leave it to you."

Alison set the book down on an end table. "No," she said. "Why don't you elaborate, Mr. Shaw? Dr. Preston told me things. What about you? Why not tell me about how you don't want Dana Mallory to kill me, but it's not your fault if he does."

Shaw ran a thin tongue across his lips. "Don't get riled."

She picked up the book again. "Well, I am riled. I'm riled about the whole week. I still have bad dreams."

"About what?" he snarled.

She caught the bitterness in his voice. "What do you mean?"

Shaw leaned forward, holding the magazine open across his knees. "Bad dreams about what? Are you in high school?"

"I'll be a senior this fall," she said.

"Uh-huh. And you have it rough. You have it really rough, don't you?"

She was becoming worried. "I don't follow you."

"I don't have any sympathy. I have bad dreams, Miss Thorne. I have nightmares, every night. *When* I fall asleep. Mostly, I have insomnia. I watch the sun rise. That's supposed to be pretty romantic."

Suddenly, she remembered mornings she'd spent on beaches, watching the sunrise; barefoot, the sun a morning blaze rippling over the ocean.

"It can be," she said.

"Well, it isn't romantic when you've been pacing the room, and you're exhausted. And you've taken two, maybe three tranquilizers, and you have a splitting headache and a vital meeting at ten and your mind and body are shot."

She listened to the heavy silence. "I don't know what to say."

"You wouldn't. Because you're not in any trouble. Not real trouble. You don't have your career, your life on the line."

"And you do?"

He leaned toward her. "That's right. I do. I'm a good lawyer, Miss Thorne. An A-1 lawyer. You name the merger, the deal, the big names, and I was there. I made billions for my clients. I was on top."

His face glowed with a fine perspiration. "What happened?" Alison asked.

"I blew one job," he said huskily. "One lousy job. Except it was a merger between Universal Imports and the American General Corporation. Multinationals, controlling half the resources in America, half the undeveloped countries in the world. My client was Universal. I was doing fine. But the magazines came to me. *Newsweek, Fortune, Time.* Suddenly, I was a cover story. They threw questions at me. I felt really *good*, you understand?

"I told them too much. I let slip a bit of classified information. It just came out. I didn't even notice it at the time. But it blew up. Scandal, Miss Thorne. Splashed over the financial pages. Acute embarrassment for the corporations. Retreats, stammered explanations. I was fired. Now I'm washed up, finished at the age of forty-five. A has-been."

Alison winced at a sudden gust of wind against the house. "I'm sorry," she said.

"Not quite as sorry as I am," Shaw joked bleakly. "But you see, I haven't slashed my wrists. Haven't taken an overdose of barbiturates. Why do you suppose I haven't, Miss Thorne?"

"You're too smart," she said.

He laughed hollowly. "Don't be an idiot, girl. Dying is smart when you gain nothing by staying alive. No, I'm alive because there is hope. A glimmer of hope. You see, my long friendship with Gordon Foxworth was not in vain. I'm the executor of his estate."

Alison caught her breath. She wondered if Gramps knew.

"You look shocked," Shaw said. "Why not? An evil character like me. But I'm good. Good enough to qualify for the legal plum of the century. I'll be in the news again, but I'll be the hero. I'll be in charge of the Foxworth holdings. A corporation nearly as big as Universal. They'll come to me, then. Crawling. Except there are catches.

"Catch one, Miss Thorne, is that I must keep this a secret until Foxworth dies. Gordon wants to keep 'em guessing, to spread confusion. He doesn't want me approached. I can't tell anybody how powerful I'm going to be.

"Catch two, Miss Thorne, is that Gordon Foxworth lives. Healthy as a horse at sixty-five. He might live for ten more years, or twenty, or even thirty. And meanwhile, I sink into the gutter. I go to work for small law firms, I starve. The only possible way out for me is Gordon Foxworth's untimely death. If he dies now, I make it."

Shaw sat back, lit a cigarette. Alison watched him, stunned.

"If you're really clever, Miss Thorne," Shaw said. "You may discern a motive. A motive, perhaps, for shooting at Gordon Foxworth on a dark night. For wanting him dead. You do see it, don't you?"

"Yes," Alison said softly. "I see it. But, of course, you didn't do it."

Shaw smiled. "Of course. You're a bright girl. I didn't do it. I thought of doing it, but I didn't have the guts. Except that Gordon may not understand that. Gordon will be smart enough to figure my motive. He may, in fact, be convinced of it. And he may, in his lonely psychosis, decide to punish me, to feed me to the dogs. Without allowing me a trial. He may kill me."

Alison wished that Jeff were here. "Why are you telling this to me? Do you think I'm the key? Everyone else does."

Shaw laughed quietly. "Not surprising. Yes, I do think you're important, Miss Thorne. I think, at least, that you have influence with Gordon Foxworth. I wish you'd use the influence. Try to disabuse him of any notions of my guilt. And, as I said, don't go into the woods."

"Why does Mallory want to kill me?" Alison asked.

Shaw drew on his cigarette. "I don't betray confidences any more. That got me in trouble once."

He unwound his narrow frame from the chair and stubbed out the cigarette in an ashtray. "Help me," he said to Alison. "I don't want anyone to die this week."

He left the room and she sat alone, trying to understand. This house was filled with desperate people, and she'd suffered terrors that she hadn't expected. And maybe they were all right. She began to believe that it did all revolve around her.

She caught a movement at the edge of her vision. Jill had

materialized in the foyer, stood now by the front window, silhouetted against a cloudy sky. The clouds had moved in rapidly, silently, like assassins. Jill looked like a part of the clouds, a lithe witch who had summoned them.

Ted drifted into the foyer, from somewhere in the house. He held a half-smoked cigarette in his fingers and stopped to take a drag, grimacing in distaste. He came to Alison, and ground out the cigarette in an ashtray.

"All by yourself?" he asked.

"Until now."

"How about a walk outside?"

A cold spot congealed in her stomach, for no good reason.

"With you?"

Ted nodded. "Yeah. Me and Jill."

"Is anything wrong?"

Ted blinked impassively. "No. We just want to talk to you."

Alison glanced over at Jill. She remained staring out the window, aloof. Alison felt oddly trapped, though she was sure they wouldn't hurt her if she refused.

She tried to look unruffled as she stood. "Okay," she said. "I have nothing else to do."

Ted escorted her to the front door and opened it. She stepped out into a hot, clinging evening, sweltering under dark clouds. A lurid green glow lit the estate. Birds fell hushed and only the hum of insects disturbed the sickly calm.

Jill came out and rushed down the front steps, as if eager to be away from the house. Alison followed, with Ted behind her. She was deeply afraid. Just jumpy, she decided. It had been a scary week, and she saw ghosts at every corner.

Jill's face caught the half light, and it made her beautiful. An enigmatic smile flickered across her features. "This is peaceful, isn't it?"

Alison nodded. She'd always felt inferior around Jill. She

wondered why Martin didn't fall for *her* if he was looking for love. She laughed to herself. Now he could.

Jill moved across the open meadow, toward the forest. Ted stayed at Alison's side. Alison suddenly felt under guard. She wished Jeff would appear.

Jill halted, abruptly, and stood motionless in the grass. Bony in wraparound shirt and jeans, she seemed a part of the landscape, as necessary to it as the forest and the clouds.

"They buy and sell this," she said, and Alison had to strain to hear.

"Who does?" she asked.

Jill snapped her head and caught Alison's eyes. "Foxworth. His friends. They take what they want."

Alison wet her lips. "I know. I don't like it either."

"Nobody likes it," Jill said. "But they allow it. We *won't* allow it."

So this was a campaign speech. "I know. Martin wants to stop some of these big businessmen from grabbing up public land."

Jill made a cathedral of her fingers and dipped her head so that her lips touched her nails. She seemed to be smiling, but Alison couldn't tell. Ted lit another cigarette, and the scrape of his match made a jumpy noise.

Jill turned to face Alison. "You've made Martin very upset. He's terribly hurt."

"I'm sorry. I didn't ask him to feel that way about me."

"You're hollow," Jill said accusingly. "There's nothing to you. You just take up room. We can't do anything about that. But you owe us something. You owe Martin a victory."

Alison had trouble breathing. The mugginess filled her mouth. "What are you trying to say?"

"Go back to him," Jill insisted. "Lie to him. I don't care. Give him back his strength."

"That's ridiculous," Alison protested. "He was campaigning against land-grabbing before he met me. I didn't give him ideals."

"He is in love with you," Jill hissed. "Stupidly. You must be in love with him. You don't have a choice."

Alison felt a knot of anger grow. "Yes, I do have a choice. I don't love Martin. He can handle that."

Jill moved through the grass. She came quite close to Alison, her face filled with a sudden ruthlessness.

"You don't know me," Jill said. "Martin is too nice; I'm not. He's popular, he can get elected. But we have to do more. The rich are taking apart the world. Nobody stops them. We have to stop them. You can't outvote them or legislate against them because they own everything. You have to hurt them. Get rid of them. Kill them."

"I don't understand you."

"Yes you do. We'll get Martin elected, but we'll do more than that. We'll do whatever is necessary. Because we have to win."

Alison tried to control her trembling. "I take this as a threat."

"This is fact. You are going back to Martin. Like I said, you have no choice."

Jill tossed her hair and in seconds was yards away from Alison, jogging back to the house, all limbs and flowing torso. Ted smoked in silence.

Alison looked at him. He seemed almost comforting. Solid, phlegmatic, looking older than his thirty years.

"That was cute," Alison said. "Did she think I would listen?"

Ted nodded. "Yes."

"I'm sorry, then. She's lost touch with reality. I'll work very hard for Martin, but his misplaced emotions are his problem. And my life belongs to me."

Ted exhaled smoke into the darkening air. "Your choice."

"Is that a threat, too?" She shook her head and looked at him angrily and sadly. "I can't figure you out," she said. "Jill's a fanatic. She looks like a fanatic. But you don't fit. Veteran, square haircut, quiet guy. You look like you should work for an ad agency."

"I did work for an ad agency," Ted said, unsmiling. "I hated it. I wanted something physical. Like the war."

She searched his face. "Was it rough for you?"

"Rougher for other guys."

She was aware of a dark power in his voice. "You saw a lot of action?"

His eyes remained locked on hers, while he took the cigarette from his dry lips. "I killed people."

She struggled against the implicit horror of his words.

"I'm going in," he said.

He dropped the butt to the grass and crushed it with his heel. He turned toward the house. She took a step toward him.

"All right. You shot at Uncle Gordon on that dark road. Am I right?"

Ted kept walking, his muscular body swaying slightly from the shoulders.

"Then you're like the others, like Preston and Shaw, making me aware of your motive. Why? What am I supposed to do? What are my lines?"

He was quite a distance from her, and she realized that her words were falling on the heavy air.

She avoided Jeff for the rest of the evening, wanting to think. Jeff wasn't hard to avoid; he nodded to her once, and went up to his room to work on his story. So, short of knocking at his door, there was no real way to see him. That freed her to sit in the foyer, pretending to read, filled with a deep foreboding. She didn't like being terrorized, not by Mallory or the others, and certainly not by the likes of Jill.

Martin kept a low profile as well, and the hours passed tensely, as a light rain fell outside. Finally, Alison was tired enough to go to sleep. She'd escaped today, but there would be tomorrow. She would not pretend to like Martin, for sure. So now she had to dodge Ted and Jill, and be wary of their vengeful acts. She was angry as well as worried. What could Jill and Ted do to her? Garrote her on a hidden path? It was insane.

She undressed quickly and slipped under the blankets with relief. Exhaustion seeped through her bones as she relaxed, and she forgot the idea of reading in bed. She reached over to the tangerine-colored lamp and switched it off, plunging the room into darkness. She listened to the wind of her own breath for a long time, not willing to sift through events or meanings.

The bedroom door opened with a sharp click. Alison's eyes flew open and she caught her breath. The door squeaked as it admitted the intruder, squeaked again as it closed. She heard the tumblers fall and the door was closed. She heard ragged masculine breathing in the darkness.

She tried to decide what to do. She could scream, or she could pretend to be asleep. Unless this was Mallory, and he was intending to suffocate her with her pillow.

The intruder crossed the room and stood at the foot of her bed. Her blood sang in her ears.

She was suddenly aware of her clock, ticking thunderously. She itched everywhere. The intruder was not moving, just watching her. She realized that her eyes were open and that he could see that in the darkness. He knew she was awake.

She moistened her mouth. "Who is it?" she whispered.

The intruder came around to the side of the bed. She stiffened under her blanket. "Jeff?"

He was looming over her now, a vague shape in the night. She stared at him, wanting to cry out, not allowing it. He moved his hands in an odd way, as if clenching and unclenching them.

"Don't scream," he said suddenly.

She recognized the voice, but for a moment she couldn't place it. "Mallory?" she asked.

"Shut up. I can kill ye with my hands."

Murdoch. Her heart sank. How stupid of her to expect him to stay away. To accept Uncle Gordon's precipitous move after all those years of service.

"What do you want?" she asked.

"I came back."

"How did you get in?"

Murdoch chuckled, or what passed for a chuckle. It was a hoarse, sepulchral sound. "Ye can't get help like me any more. No loyalty. I had some money saved up, over the years. I paid William to take me for a ride, turn around, and come back. Only I was on the floor in the back of the car. I snuck out, and I hid in the woods."

So that was why William smiled this morning. Not because he was evilly glad to see Murdoch fired. Because he was making a buck and ripping off the boss.

"Why did you come to me?" she asked.

"I want my job back," Murdoch said.

"I can't get it for you."

"Ye're lying."

"Listen." She sat up in bed, unable to see Murdoch clearly. Anger mingled with her fear. "I have no influence with Uncle Gordon. They all think I do. Dr. Preston. Mr. Shaw. But I don't. He won't let me go home any more than the others. And I've been attacked by Dana Mallory, almost killed. So he's not a very nice uncle. I didn't get you fired, Murdoch."

Murdoch clapped a hand on her shoulder, forced her back. She was surprised at his strength. He sat on the bed, his fingers near her throat.

"Ye got me fired, all right. I don't know how, or why. But it's you. He tells me everything. I know more about Gordon Foxworth than anybody on earth. But he didn't tell me about this party. They're all here for a reason, and ye're the cause of it."

"How?" Her voice was an echo.

Murdoch's eyes glittered in the half light. "He started to talk about you. He brought out family albums, old pictures. He spent whole nights in the den, looking at those pictures. He wanted ye here this week. And he wanted the others to be here with ye. Now ye've got to find out why."

"No." She was surprised at her own resentment. "I'm not a detective. Let Uncle Gordon tell me if he has a reason. I don't like to play games."

"It's not a game." Murdoch tightened his grip and, in panic, she felt her windpipe cut off. He leaned close to her and, madly, she wondered if he would kill her. But he only searched her face.

"He's dead serious," Murdoch insisted. "He fired me last night, and it wasn't a joke. He's changed. Because of you, everything's different. I want it the same as it was."

"But you can't kill people," she said, fighting for air.

He abruptly released his grip. He sat up rigidly. "I never tried to kill anyone."

"You didn't tell me about the dogs—"

"I forgot."

"You let the dogs loose when Jeff was outside."

"I didn't know he was outside," Murdoch hissed. "And I let the dogs loose because I always do in the afternoons. I checked to see nobody was outside. And anyway, I was *told* to let 'em loose."

Alison was interested now. "Who told you?"

Murdoch half smiled. "Martin Young. He said Foxworth had given him the message. And I was stupid enough to believe it."

Alison's pulse pounded now, where his hands had circled her neck. "Why didn't you say that before?"

"Young would deny it. And Mr. Foxworth would have fired me anyway. But it's the truth. And I suffered for it. You owe me my job."

Alison tried to make sense of it, but her head spun. "I have to think." She said.

Murdoch stood. "Yes. Think. But don't think too long."

With a rush of wind as the door opened and closed, Murdoch was gone.

12 • Surprises in the Woods

Alison resented the hot sunlight pouring through the windows of the den. The dazzling brightness fell across the animal heads, the floor, the furniture, and her own hair, making it glow. She wished for a moment that it would rain, making it reasonable to stay indoors.

Ed Ginger carried in a tray with a bowl of cereal, juice, milk, and toast. He set the tray on a table before her.

"Here you go," he said.

"Thanks."

He stood near her, watching as she drank her juice. "Any particular reason that you wanted to eat alone?"

"Yes," she said quietly. "I didn't want to see anybody."

"Pretty rough to do that here."

"I know. But I can try."

Ed sensed her bitterness and retreated to the bar. He took a cloth and began to polish the bar top, inventing motion to avoid embarrassment.

"Don't even want to see that reporter?" he asked.

She gave him a withering look. "No."

"Caught between him and Martin Young?"

She shook her head at the obtuseness of people. "Are you doing a gossip column?"

Ed leaned on the bar and cocked an eye at her. "I'm just interested, Alison. I like you. I think you're a terrific kid and I want to see you happy."

She felt chastised. "Thanks."

"Well, I owe you an apology anyway. I was nasty to you a couple of days ago."

"I'm getting used to nastiness."

"The thing is, I'm a little worried myself. The boss has kept us in the dark about this convention, and I don't care for all the indiscriminate gunplay. So forgive me for being edgy."

She paused in her eating, which was halfhearted to begin with. She hadn't told anybody about Murdoch's visit last night. She was no longer afraid of Murdoch, but she did feel pity for him.

"I forgive you. You're the only one who's been decent to me."

"I like you," he said again. "I thought your uncle liked you, too. Now I don't know."

"Neither do I."

Ed chewed his lip, searching for words. "Alison, why is Foxworth doing this?"

She stared at him. "You too?"

"What does that mean?"

"They all think I know," she said. "They come to me and expect me to solve it for them."

Ed snapped the cloth to clean out the dust. "It seems logical that you'd know. You're his great-niece."

"But I'm part of his game."

"It also seems logical that you're the reason for this mad tea party. He invited you and surrounded you with a gang of nasty characters. Why you?"

"All right," she said. "Why?"

Ed shrugged. "Blank. You're the wild card. You're the one who doesn't fit. Unless you shot at him."

Alison laughed. "No, I didn't shoot at him."

"Which makes you odd man out. Little Nell in the nest of thieves. Alison, think about it. If he hasn't told you why, doesn't that make something clear?"

"No," she said.

Ed came around the bar. "He wants you to dope it out. He wants you to make sense of it. And he's giving you a week."

"Well, I *can't* make sense of it. I'm scared and I'm angry and I want to go home. I'll wait out the week—if I survive. He can tell me then."

"But it'll be too late."

"For what?"

"For you." Ed went to her, pulled over a chair, and perched at the edge of the cushion. "It's a test, Alison. Don't you see that? He's got you picked out to pick up the marbles when he dies. But you have to be worthy."

Click. Two theories coming together: Dad's, Eric's. Get the dope on Fallon, do well, and inherit. "My father thought that."

"You father was right. It makes sense. It's the only answer that makes sense. And your time is running out."

Her stomach turned over. "It's impossible. There are too many things . . . it's not that simple."

"No," Ed agreed. "I think Foxworth has a tiger by the tail and doesn't know it. I think there are things happening that he never expected. Foxworth has lit a fuse and the bomb goes off at the end of this week. Unless you defuse it."

"What about you?" she asked. "You're a lot more capable than I am."

"I've been trying," he said, "but he's stacked the cards for you. You have the key to everything, not me."

She stared at the rapidly cooling oatmeal, a sense of unreality upon her. "This is insane," she whispered. "I'm a normal healthy American girl, not a whiz kid. I get into dangerous situations sometimes, but not situations like *this*."

"You're in one," Ed pointed out.

She looked at him. "I don't know what to do. I wouldn't know where to start."

"It's been started for you. Mallory. Murdoch. The attack on Martin Young, and the attack on Jeff. I'd do some hard thinking, Alison. And fast."

She turned away, stared out the window at the blazing landscape. "Why did he make it my responsibility?"

"I don't know," Ed admitted. "He knows you're a capable girl, and you've come through some rough adventures. You've got the brains and the grit, and you've got to use them. Or somebody is going to die before the week is up, and you'll put the bullet into him."

She stood up, shaking. "Don't put it that way."

"I have to."

She moved toward the door, shaken, and nearly tripped as Mallory filled the entryway. He stepped into the room, went to the bar.

"Bourbon, neat," he said.

Ed went to pour the drink. Alison stood for a long moment, breathing evenly. Terror rippled through her whenever she saw Mallory now. She took a step toward the door.

"Hold it," Mallory said.

She stopped. Mallory drank down his bourbon and pursed his lips. "Come here," he said.

She turned, looked at him, hating him violently. He gestured with the empty shot glass. She crossed the room, avoiding Ed Ginger's eyes, until she stood near him. She could smell the liquor on his breath.

"Haven't seen you for a while," he said.

She didn't answer. Ed Ginger turned his attention to polishing glasses. Mallory twisted his head to watch Ed.

"Why don't you take a break, fella?"

Ed turned, balancing on the balls of his feet, hands loose beside him. "Foxworth found out about what you did to Alison in the pool."

Mallory sat down his glass. "And?"

"And I'm making sure it doesn't happen again. So why don't *you* take the break?"

Mallory moved with suddenness and startling violence. His hand closed around Ed's shirt collar and Ed was pulled over the bar, skimming glasses to the floor, where they shattered. Ed fell, crying out. Mallory waited for Ed to attempt to stand, and then cracked a hand across the side of his jaw. Ed grunted and fell back, thudding among the broken glass.

Mallory stood over him, breathing rapidly.

It had happened quickly, and Alison could not focus. She tried to go to Ed to help him, but Mallory turned and stood in her way. "Preston and Shaw came to see you, didn't they?" he demanded.

Alison just stared at Mallory.

"Full of confessions. Letting you know they didn't shoot at Foxworth. Really touching."

Alison backed away, aware of the real possibility of being hurt, badly hurt, by Mallory. Mallory made no move toward her. But the threat was there in the readiness of his strong body.

"I'll tell you what," Mallory said. "I'll add my own confession. Make it three out of three. Except I'll make it short. Those other two, they bend your ear. Smart guys. College boys. Not me. I dropped out in the eighth grade. Sold scrap with my old man. I drifted around, job to job. I did a hitch in the Marines. That's where I learned how to shoot. I came back with nothing to do. That happens sometimes. The military is a great thing. You don't have to think. They make the decisions and you carry them out. You aim, you pull the trigger, you take what's coming. But back home, it's tougher. You have to make it on your own.

"I couldn't hack it. I was a dropout, a bum. I took odd jobs, one in a lumberyard. Met a girl from a nice suburb of Long Island. Married her. She was sick of nothing guys and liked my style. We didn't last long. But she had money, and I used it. I went in with another guy, and started building houses. Spot. Went into hock over our ears. He handled the loans. I handled the men and the equipment."

Ed stirred, and Mallory rolled him over with the toe of his shoe. "I made it work," he said. "We got rich. I got to know people like Foxworth, and Shaw, and Preston. They never liked me a lot. But they did business with me. They used my dough for their rotten deals, so they put up with me. Things were pretty good.

"Until my partner went off the road in his Mercedes and burned to death. Then I found out that half my business was owned by the mob. And they expected heavy payment. I won't do it. They've already sabotaged me. Trucks with cut brake linings, fires in my lumberyards, wrecked building sites, workers attacked. They'll get rougher. And I'm on the short end."

He stopped abruptly, went behind the bar and poured himself another drink. Alison saw that Ed Ginger was starting to revive. He bled through his shirt, and his jaw was already swollen and discolored. She turned to Mallory.

"Where's the rest of it?" she asked. "Your motive for shooting at Uncle Gordon? The others had motives."

Mallory drained the glass. "I don't have a motive. I was working on Gordon Foxworth. For a loan. Enough to buy off these gorillas until I could figure a way out. He didn't like it, but he was weakening. I think he digs me in a weird way.

I walk around in garbage, fighting the world out there. He picks pansies in his garden. It bothers him. I'm an alter ego. So I never wanted him dead. I want him alive. And I want to know who doesn't."

Shapes that had been floating in her mind, senseless and frightening, began to coalesce. Despite her fear and revulsion at Mallory's behavior, her brain worked.

"You suspect your partners?"

"Maybe. Do you?"

"Or maybe you suspect Andrew Fallon. Why?"

Mallory came around the bar. "You figure it out."

She pushed back an errant hair with her hand. "That's what you want me to do, isn't it? Figure it out. It's very important to you that I find the answer."

Mallory's eyes glittered. "That's right."

"Important enough to threaten me and terrorize me. To scare me into doing your detective work. Because *you're* scared, right?"

Mallory laughed. "You're slow, but you catch on."

Alison wet her lips. "Why don't you figure it our yourself!"

Mallory started to speak, but she silenced him with her next words.

"No, don't tell me," she said. "I know. Because Ed Ginger told me the same thing. You *can't* figure it out. You've tried, and you come up empty. But I'm the key to everything. I don't fit in with the group, so obviously I'm the reason for Uncle Gordon's game. I have the inside track. Everybody needs me."

She was full of pure anger and it gave her strength. "You could have told me, Mallory. You didn't have to come out swinging. You didn't have to do this to Ed."

Mallory glanced at Ed. "Sure I did. You had to know how things stood. Your great-uncle got us together, but he's out of it now. He can't control us. You can't be protected. Not from me. Not from anybody."

"So you'll kill me if I don't help you."

"It's possible," Mallory said. "And somebody else may kill you if you *do* help me. I'm going to squeeze you between those two walls until there's no place for you to go."

"In two days I go home," she said.

"Do you?"

He kicked aside a shard of glass with his foot and left the room. Alison hurried to Ed, knelt by him. Ed's eyes opened heavily. A trickle of blood had dried at his mouth.

"Are you okay?" she asked.

"What I need," he said thickly, "is a bouncer."

He leaned against her for support and she helped him to his feet. He placed a beefy hand on the bar and touched his jaw with a finger.

"Ouch," he said wryly. "What did he have to tell you that was so important?"

"Pretty much what you told me just before. Except he was less subtle."

Ed's eyes narrowed. "Obviously, you got to him."

"Obviously, I'm the girl of the hour. I have a houseful of desperate men panting after me to solve their problems. Me, who's trying to get her own life set up."

Ed kicked at the loose glass. "Well, some have greatness thrust upon them, as the saying goes. *I* have a stake in this now."

"How so?" she asked.

"You have to find the answers before Mallory breaks the other side of my face."

He hustled off for a broom and Alison surveyed the wreckage of the den, and of the morning. A new set of emotions struggled inside her. Mallory appeared in a different light. She wasn't quite ready to weep for him, but he was a man in trouble, not a man making trouble. It was possible that Preston and Shaw were afraid of Mallory, but they'd given him *carte blanche* to harass her, to force her to get the truth before the week was up.

Mallory wanted Uncle Gordon alive. If his story was true. Somebody wanted Uncle Gordon dead. Somebody also tried to kill Martin. And Jeff.

But *Martin* had ordered Murdoch to loose the dogs. According to Murdoch. And Martin had been out in the woods with his gun, appearing at the proper moment to save Jeff. Why? Was there an arrangement between Martin and Jeff?

Alison found herself driven by determination. She was at the brink of something. There were so many things to consider. The Arab headdress found by Jeff. The mystery man stalking her through the woods. The unknown visitor at the hunters' cabin. Today was Thursday. In a day or two more, the fuse would burn up. And somebody would be dead. Possibly her.

She smiled ruefully. If Eric could see her now. *He* was the one who was supposed to be so adventurous and daring.

The smile faded. She was deep into a mess and couldn't find her way out. Gramps and Dad would not suspect that anything wrong was going on, and Eric was sailing in the Caribbean. She wanted to be out of here, back home, safe, or even out in the open facing another Soviet spy. At least she'd have room to run. She glanced out at the hot sunlight. It was time to be outside.

She ducked under the cold surface of the lake, arched and wriggled through the water, fishlike, urging the chill and the pure physical sensation on herself, seeking to escape at least for a moment, to regroup and think clearly. She opened her eyes and pondered the clear blue silence, the smoky mud of the lake bottom, the waving plants. She stayed under, propelling herself strongly, until her lungs screamed for relief. She surfaced and gulped air, treading water. Now her eyes cleared and she saw Jeff at the shore. He wore a black bathing suit and was peeling off his shirt. He waved to her, and waded into the water.

She disliked herself as she swam away, cursing her cowardice. There was no reason to ignore Jeff, to run from him. Jill was a fanatic, and Martin would no doubt chew her out if he knew what she'd done. But logic and reason never seemed to prevail in this place, and she could not prevent herself from fleeing.

She heard Jeff call to her, his voice thin over the distance. Her feet clawed, found purchase on the soft mud. She half waded, half swam until she was out of the water. Slipping on rocks, she hurried to the grassy bank.

She reached the shore, turned to look for Jeff. He swam determinedly, chasing her. She waited until he was in the middle of the lake, then ran, doubling back toward the house. Perspiration sheeted her wet body in the lime bathing suit, and humidity was a mask over her face. She cried out angrily as she ran, realizing that she was being ridiculous.

She stopped, near the path into the woods—her path. Jeff had changed direction, was still after her. She became annoyed at his insistence. She did not *want* to be with him.

She glanced at the house, at the woods. She chose the woods. She wasn't certain why. Maybe answers waited in the green forest. But there was not time for analysis.

The forest was little cooler than the open meadow. The leaves hung still and dark green, the earth heavy and dry. Twigs broke and animals crashed away from her as she passed the dogs. The shepherds looked up sharply, but otherwise didn't move. Barefoot, hair still wet and clinging to her shoulders, Alison slowed to a breathless jog. She threw back her head as her throat burned.

She stopped, finally, blinded by her own perspiration. She wiped her eyes with a grimy hand and wished fervently for the lake again, and the air-conditioned house. She was in an oven. Insects droned angrily, alive and vicious in this heat, and she slapped at mosquitoes that swarmed around her, tormenting her.

She listened with a strange terror to the rasp of her own breath. This was absurd. She had to go back to Jeff and tell him. She needed his help. For one demented moment, she had believed herself capable of solving the mystery. There was a perverse need to prove herself to Mallory, to Ed, to Preston and Shaw. And to Uncle Gordon. But the moment had passed and left the sheer weight of helplessness.

She heard a branch snap, and gasped. She listened, her face glistening in the dank shadows. Her lips were slightly parted, her teeth bared. The sound came again, with a rustling. There was somebody in the woods, following her.

She felt suddenly vulnerable in the bathing suit, with no weapon or protection. Now there were more footsteps, but she couldn't place them. She moved a few steps further up the path, deeper into the woods. The noises came from behind her. It was definite now. So she couldn't double back. She had to try for the hunters' cabin, and pray that the phone worked.

She walked slowly and deliberately, her legs aching to stretch and run. But if she ran, she might encourage a shot. Her back quivered. She felt faint and her mouth and throat were parched. Her discomfort was acute, aggravated by the gnats and mosquitoes that refused to leave her.

She wondered if Mallory were following her. Wondered what she could do, even if she reached the cabin. He'd never allow her to pick up the phone. But why would he want to kill her after going through such a lengthy speech earlier this morning?

Her mind was racing. She was not accomplishing anything this way. She moved on, her feet hurting from the rocks and underbrush. Her wet bathing suit clung uncomfortably to her body, the straps biting into her shoulders. She daydreamed vividly of dry clothes, cold lemonade, Gramps's chocolate chip cookies.

There was a sudden flurry of footsteps, and Alison turned. She saw the figure now, tall and slim, young and male. Dressed in a dark brown uniform.

"William," she said, more loudly than she'd intended.

The chauffeur stopped and looked at her, face frozen. She took a step toward him, and he broke from the woods, ran full tilt down the path.

She watched him until he was gone, and allowed reflief to flood her. She had no answer for William's presence. Perhaps he'd stalked her the last time, when she'd come here with Jeff. She'd have to talk to him. Maybe he was spying for Uncle Gordon. It seemed a good guess.

The hunters' cabin was around the next curve, which made her decide to visit, to freshen herself before trekking back to the house. She broke into a gentle trot. The cabin appeared and she suffered a small twinge, half expecting to see a menacing figure.

She tried the door, found it open. She stepped inside, closed the door behind her and sighed in shuddering gratitude that the insects were gone, at least for the moment. She glanced around and headed for the bathroom.

She heard the noise behind her too late to wonder about it. There was only time enough to spin around, to see the barrel of the rifle aimed at her throat, to see who held the gun.

Laura Fallon advanced a few steps, her face peaked and ash white. She wore a shirt and white shorts, her legs scratched and bruised from tramping through the woods. She was grimy, and her mouth trembled.

Alison tried to decide how to handle it. She couldn't imagine that Laura would shoot. Yet Laura had the gun.

"You're always barging in," Laura said huskily.

"You were here last time," Alison said. "You went out the window."

"Yes," Laura said. "Did you have to come then for a tryst?"

"It wasn't a tryst," Alison said, watching the gun, fascinated by it, and by the potential it represented.

"I'll kill you," Laura said without emotion, "if I have to."

"What do you want me to do?"

"Leave. Go back and don't tell anybody I'm here."

"All right."

Laura choked back a sudden and unexpected sob. "You won't do it. You'll tell them I'm here. I can't let you leave."

"You can't kill me," Alison said.

"Oh, yes," Laura said. "Yes I can. I'm going to kill three others. I can kill you. After the first, it doesn't matter."

"Why?" Alison asked.

Laura hefted the gun. It was obviously heavy for her. "To save my husband, and myself. They'll think it was an accident. Those men are always hunting. Everyone will think they shot each other."

"No," Alison said. "They can tell where the bullets came from. The angle, the gun, everything."

Laura looked at her. She stared at the gun in her hands, as if seeing it for the first time. The gun fell and Alison winced at the crash, half expecting it to go off. Laura covered her face.

Alison moved swiftly, scooping up the rifle and holding onto it. Laura was crying voluminously, without sound. "What is it?" Alison asked.

Laura spoke almost to herself, in a steady voice, through the tears which did not abate. "I hate this life. I always have. I don't like politics. I don't like appearing in public, smiling when I don't want to smile, hearing my husband vilified, receiving hate mail, reading editorials. . . . I married Andrew because he was sincere and kind to me and didn't make demands."

Laura looked up, blinking her wet eyes. "You can't imagine how I hated it. I never knew it would be so crowded and horrible. And when he made the deal, I knew I had to help him, or there would be scandal, and I couldn't take that. I couldn't."

Alison held the gun vertically, resting the stock on the floor. "What deal, Mrs. Fallon?"

Laura seemed almost surprised that Alison didn't know. "Why, the deal with Gordon and those three men. With Mallory, and Dr. Preston, and Cory Shaw. They came to Andrew late this spring. In May, I think. They came to our home and they had Andrew in the den for a long time. I heard the conversation, although they spoke low so I wouldn't hear. But I have excellent hearing.

"They were offering Andrew a deal. They would sabotage Martin Young's campaign, hurt him, make sure he lost the election, if Andrew would help pass legislation enabling them to do illegal things with land—Long Island land, New England land—all over."

"Did your husband say yes?" Alison asked.

Laura clasped her hands together. "Of course he said yes. What else could he say? They told him to think it over that night, and he called them from his office. Now they're all here together. They must be out to hurt Martin Young. That's why he was shot at. I have to prevent it. I can't let Andrew become involved in this."

Alison fought her racing heartbeat, and tried to think clearly. "So you decided to kill Mallory, Preston, and Shaw. And maybe Uncle Gordon. But you wouldn't have done it."

"Yes. I have to do it."

"But you wouldn't have. You know it."

Laura shook her head, in agony. "I don't know what to do. I don't want Andrew to win that way. To be owned by these men."

"Why don't we talk to him?"

"No. He doesn't know I overheard him."

Alison picked up the gun, held it with revulsion. "He doesn't have any options right now. His hand is in the till. Maybe we can stop the sabotage by facing up to it."

Laura looked out the cabin window. "I don't know. I don't know what will happen now."

"Let's find out."

Laura allowed Alison to herd her from the cabin. She waited while Alison closed the door. The two women walked back along the path, and Alison felt foolish holding the rifle, which grew heavier each yard. She wondered what to do with this revelation. Warn Martin? Tell Uncle Gordon? Or Mallory, Preston, or Shaw? Was this Uncle Gordon's real motive—to lure Martin into a death trap? It didn't seem plausible. But nothing else did, either; only the hot forest and her own dark foreboding.

13 • More Pressures

They broke from the woods and started across the open land to the house. The sun was a white sheet in a white sky, beating down on the two women. Alison wondered what others would think, spotting her with the rifle, guarding Laura Fallon.

The house shimmered in the heat, seeming no closer as they made their way through the grass. Laura sniffled, stumbling as she walked. Nobody was outside on the terrace; to court this savage weather deliberately would be folly.

Alison felt weakened when they finally gained the house. Laura shook her head slowly.

"I can't face him, she said. Her voice was dry and thick. "I can't let him know."

"Let's discuss it inside, where it's cool."

She pushed open the door, and the cold wind of the air conditioning wrapped around her gloriously. She stood for a delicious moment, soaking up the comfort, then urged Laura to continue through the hallway. They walked into the foyer. It seemed empty at first, until Alison spied the stocky, preoccupied man seated in a high-backed chair. He stared listlessly out the front window, blinking slowly. His pale face seemed bloodless. He was a nearly ridiculous figure, in a flowered shirt and summer shorts.

"He's here," Alison said to Laura.

Laura looked at Alison, wild-eyed. "No."

Andrew Fallon twisted in his chair when he heard the voices. He stood uncertainly, trying to make sense of the bedraggled women, the gun, and Laura's ashen face.

"What's wrong?" he asked.

Laura covered her mouth with her hands. "I'm sorry," she said. "I'm sorry."

She turned and was gone before Alison could say anything to stop her. Alison was suddenly bone tired. The heat had taken more of a toll than she'd thought.

Fallon gaped at her. "I don't understand."

"Sit down," Alison said wearily. "Please."

She dragged herself into the foyer, sank into a chair, and let the room spin. Fallon sat opposite her, his eyes pleading. Alison wanted to cry, but she was drained.

"Laura was in the hunters' cabin," Alison said, resting the rifle against the wall. "She had this gun. She said she was going to shoot Dana Mallory, Dr. Preston, and Cory Shaw. Possibly Uncle Gordon too."

Fallon's face reflected his disbelief.

"She wouldn't have done it," Alison said. "She broke down when I found her. She told me about the deal, the one you made with those men. Is it true?"

Fallon sank back into his chair, his face bleak. "I'm good at denials," he said. "Political hacks like me can make an art of denials. But what's the difference now? Yes, it's true. They came to me with that deal."

"And you took it?"

Fallon smiled grimly. "No, I didn't take it. I find that hard to believe now. I've had my share of smoke-filled rooms and dirty pool. I've okayed illegal contracts, winked at crooked deals, given unfair tax breaks to corporations. I've played all the games that senators play. But suddenly, with your grandfather staking his reputation on me, I got religion. I wanted to be clean. Who knows, maybe I dreamed of being President. That's the American dream, isn't it? Every boy can become President?"

Alison felt as if her bathing suit was eating through her skin. "Laura thinks you went along."

"Yes, and so do Mallory, Preston, and Shaw. I let them think I would say yes. But I came to Gordon Foxworth instead. I told him what had happened. He listened very politely and thanked me. If he was part of the scheme, he didn't let on at that time."

Alison thought of Cory Shaw, executor of Uncle Gordon's estate. And Mallory, and Preston—close associates, friends. What had Mallory said? Alter egos.

Fallon wrenched himself erect in the chair, his eyes haunted. "This is the result. I knew it as soon as I came here, but I was too stupid to see it earlier. I actually believed that drivel about a special deal between the two of us. Cutting the others out. I was greedy, all right. And he brought me here to die."

"I can't believe that," Alison said.

"It's obvious. Mallory here. And the other two. But especially Mallory. A born killer. That ridiculous story about a shot at Foxworth on a dark night. Setting people against each other. Creating an atmosphere of distrust. Look at the accidents that have happened already. But I'm the real target. It will be listed as a hunting mishap. And nobody will say a word, because they'll know that Foxworth can get them, too. So I sit here, waiting."

He seemed relieved as he said the words. His face lost

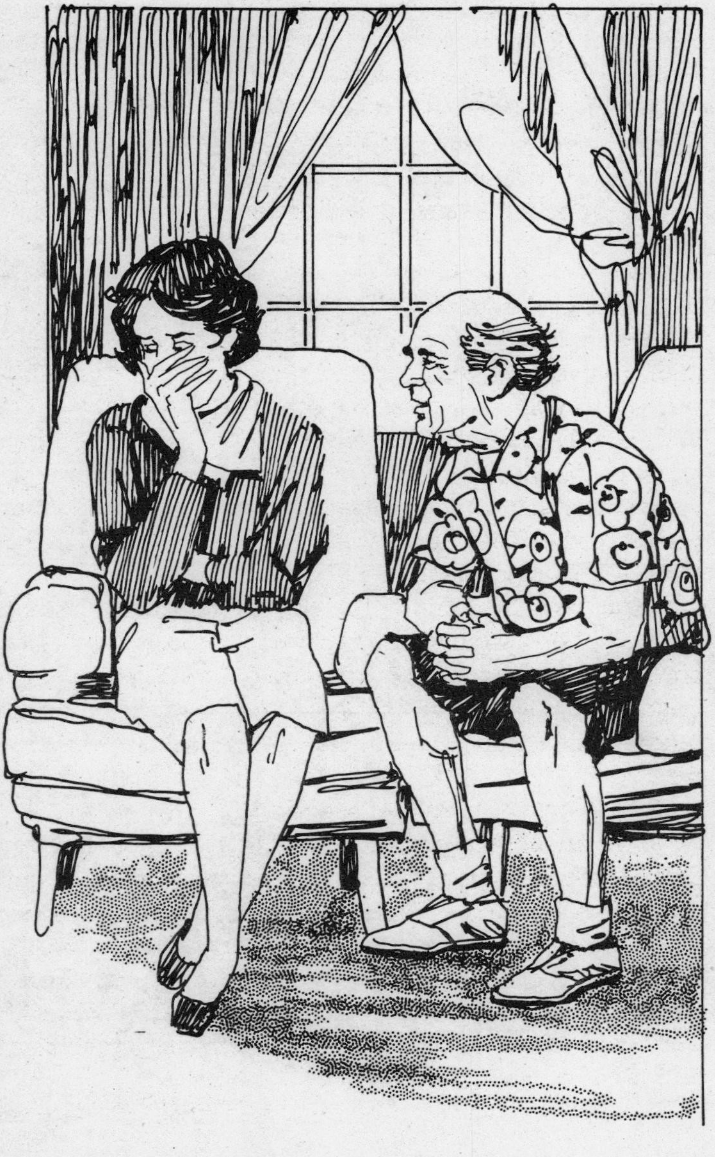

some of the strain that had pulled it out of shape. Alison tried to make sense of it.

"I know it's hard to believe," Fallon said. "Your great uncle. But he's a powerful man. He has a lot to lose and he can't risk it. I'm a threat now. I wouldn't play the game."

It *did* make sense, of course. That was the horrible part. Uncle Gordon had made a big, controversial deal with foreign businessmen—and with Mallory, Preston, and Shaw. A deal involving the sale of land, prime land, a deal so big it would need loopholes in federal legislation. So Uncle Gordon conspired with Mallory, Preston, and Shaw, and sent them to Fallon with an irresistible deal. But Fallon was a surprise. The pathetic old politician had a streak of honesty. Gramps had seen it, perhaps.

"Go to Laura," Alison said quietly. "She's very upset."

Fallon nodded. He stood up. "She's a good girl, Laura is. But she worries too much."

Alison didn't watch Fallon leave the foyer. She found that she was unable to move, and let the paralysis claim her. She realized that her bathing suit was still damp and might ruin the chair, but it hardly mattered.

She was being stupid. The Foxworth fortune hadn't been built on good intentions and Boy Scout behavior. The Foxworths had clawed and cheated and crushed people in their way. Uncle Gordon had taken on a romantic glow because of his personal tragedy and the years he'd spent in these gardens, smelling roses while Murdoch brought slippers and brandy. But there was blood on the roses and there wasn't much that was nice about Uncle Gordon. What had she expected to find? A glimpse of a monster? She'd been more than rewarded. The monsters were everywhere.

She heard the door open and close and lazily turned to look. Jeff carried his shirt, crumpled in his hand. His slim body was sunburned and damp. He wore only his black bathing suit. He stepped into the foyer and came to her. Her throat tightened.

"I put the rifle back in the gun rack," he said tautly. "It was kind of dumb to leave it leaning against the wall."

"Thanks," she said. "It *was* dumb."

"I've been searching the woods," he said. "I thought you were hurt."

"I'm not hurt," she said.

"Why did you run away from me?"

"I wanted to be alone. Why did you chase me?"

He was concealing his anger, but it simmered very near the surface. "I wanted to be with you. Just to swim and talk and maybe keep our sanity. Things like that. Helping each other out because we're both hostages here. Sound sensible?"

"Yes," she said. "It sounds sensible."

"Has anything changed that I don't know about?"

She let out a small sigh. "A lot of things have happened."

He dropped on the edge of the chair lately occupied by Fallon. "I guess so. You're toting a gun now."

She laughed quietly. "That was Laura Fallon's gun."

His eyes asked the obvious question.

"Laura Fallon was in the hunters' cabin when you showed me the *igal*. She was there again today. She was going to kill some people."

She told him everything she could remember, about Laura, and about Andrew Fallon's honesty, and the confessions of Mallory, Preston, and Shaw. About William stalking her in the woods. She told him everything except the answers, because she didn't know them.

"If you can make sense of it," she said, "good luck."

Jeff put on his shirt. "Well, somebody's lying."

"Obviously."

"I think we'll probably have to wait for Foxworth to spring his big surprise."

"And see who winds up dead?"

Jeff nodded. "Something like that."

Alison forced herself to stand, "Right now I could use a shower."

"Ditto," Jeff said, rising.

Alison tried to think of something to say, but she choked on the words. She turned, knowing that Jeff would stop her.

"Alison," he said, and she halted. She felt him come up behind her, bit her lip when she heard him exhale sadly.

"What about it?" he asked. "Is anything wrong?"

"Nothing's wrong," she said, not looking at him.

"But nothing's right either. I mean, I do sense a certain coldness."

"It's not you," she said, annoyed.

"Glad to hear it," he said. "Do you foresee a thaw in the near future?"

"I don't know," she said gently. "I can't think right now."

"I wish you would think," Jeff said. He turned her around, touching her as if she were fragile glass. She saw the honest emotion in his face, and the hurt. "You kind of got to me, Alison."

"I'm sorry," she said. "I didn't try to."

They both turned at the footstep on the stairs. Martin seemed embarrassed, hesitant about entering the room. Alison looked hard at him, at his handsome features, his glamorous assurance. He looked at her with curiosity.

Jeff still touched her arm. He looked at Martin, then at Alison. "Do you want him instead?"

Alison was appalled. "Stop it," she demanded.

Jeff let her go, and faced Martin. "She wants you," he called out.

Alison clenched her hands. "I said stop it."

Jeff looked at her, burning with anger. "Stay with the winner, baby."

He stalked across the foyer and passed Martin roughly on the stairs. Martin stared after him, then continued downstairs and came to Alison. Alison tried to compose herself. The moment had been horrible.

"What's going on?" Martin asked.

"Go away. Please."

Martin smiled at her. "I kind of caused some of this, didn't I? I didn't exactly behave like a grown-up. I'm sorry, really. Forgive me?"

She nodded. "Sure. Don't worry about it."

He continued to study her. "Is there something you're not telling me?"

She shook her head. Of course there was. She should have told him what Jill and Ted had told her to do, but he wouldn't have believed her. Besides, if he was too dense to read his own aides, that wasn't her responsibility.

Martin expelled a long breath. "Hang in there," he said.

She watched him go, with growing panic.

Alison went upstairs, and took the time for a long shower, including a hair wash. She dressed in a fresh yellow shirt and shorts, blew her hair dry, and felt human again. By the time she finished, it was late afternoon and the sun looked more buttery, less ferocious.

She went downstairs and out back to the terrace, where she was pleasantly surprised by a sprightly breeze that cleared the air of the humid rot of the morning. The forest shimmered with rustling branches, the lake reflected shattered sunlight on its surface. Alison felt refreshed.

She sat on a lounge chair in the shade and looked out at the green acreage, recapturing bits and pieces of the serenity she'd experienced on her arrival. Maybe the week would end after all. Maybe she would go home alive and forget the nightmare.

But the cold tension inside her told her differently. There would be no easy escape from Foxworth Hall. The week had built toward a climax, possibly a bloody climax, and she was part of it. She'd have to ride out the storm. And the storm of her own emotions. She'd been rudely awakened about people this week.

A lengthening shadow announced the arrival of company. She twisted to look and recoiled a little at the sight of Uncle Gordon. Tanned and fit as ever, dressed in blue, he carried two tall iced drinks.

"Fresh iced tea," he said, setting one of the glasses before her. "Brewed from fresh tea leaves, with fresh lemon and the finest cane sugar. A summer afternoon libation."

He sat beside her, sipped at his tea, gazed out at his land from hooded eyes.

"It's still beautiful," he said. "After so many years. It becomes more beautiful, in fact. When I was young, I wasted the beauty. I took it as my due and used it as a playground. Now I draw it in like breath. When there's so little time, this kind of beauty becomes almost unbearably intense. What was it Arthur Sullivan wrote in his diary, a day before he died? 'I hate to leave such a beautiful day.' "

Alison sipped at her drink, finding it strong. She didn't know how to talk to Uncle Gordon. At this point, what could she say?

"I haven't seen you much," she told him.

"I keep hidden. I was never very sociable. I'm not a very good uncle, I'm afraid."

She looked at him, intimidated by his strength and importance. "No you're not," she said, tingling a little as she said it. "You're not a very good person, either."

He pursed his lips. "I'm not surprised that you feel that way. I've made a very bad week for you."

"For a lot of people."

"Oh, come now. Some of my guests deserve a roughing up."

"But they're not the ones getting it."

Uncle Gordon's hair blew in the breeze. Close up, he looked older.

"I know," he said. "I was upset about Ed Ginger. I would have thought he could handle Mallory."

"He was taken by surprise," Alison said, shivering at the memory.

"Yes. There have been a few surprises. It's like business in a way. You arrange a set of circumstances and you're often startled when the arrangement falls apart. Then you have to play the ball where it lies. I seem to be butchering my metaphors."

Alison sat back, watching the lazy afternoon float past. "Why did you bring me iced tea?"

"Peace offering," Uncle Gordon said. "An opening gambit for some conversation."

"We can't have a conversation," she said. "You won't tell me anything. And everybody thinks I know your secrets."

Uncle Gordon smiled, mostly to himself. "I'm aware of that. Blood is thicker than water. People believe that. Despite evidence to the contrary, it is commonly thought that families stick together. All the Mafia literature helps the illusion."

"What helps *me?*" Alison asked, turning to him. "Or don't you care?"

He raised his drink. "I care very much about you, Alison. But you are sixteen years old. At sixteen, I was fighting my own battles. I didn't expect my elders to bail me out. I want no less from you."

"I've fought my own battles. But not blindfolded."

"If you're blindfolded," Uncle Gordon said, "you have to use your other senses."

There was silence between them, and she nursed the tea,

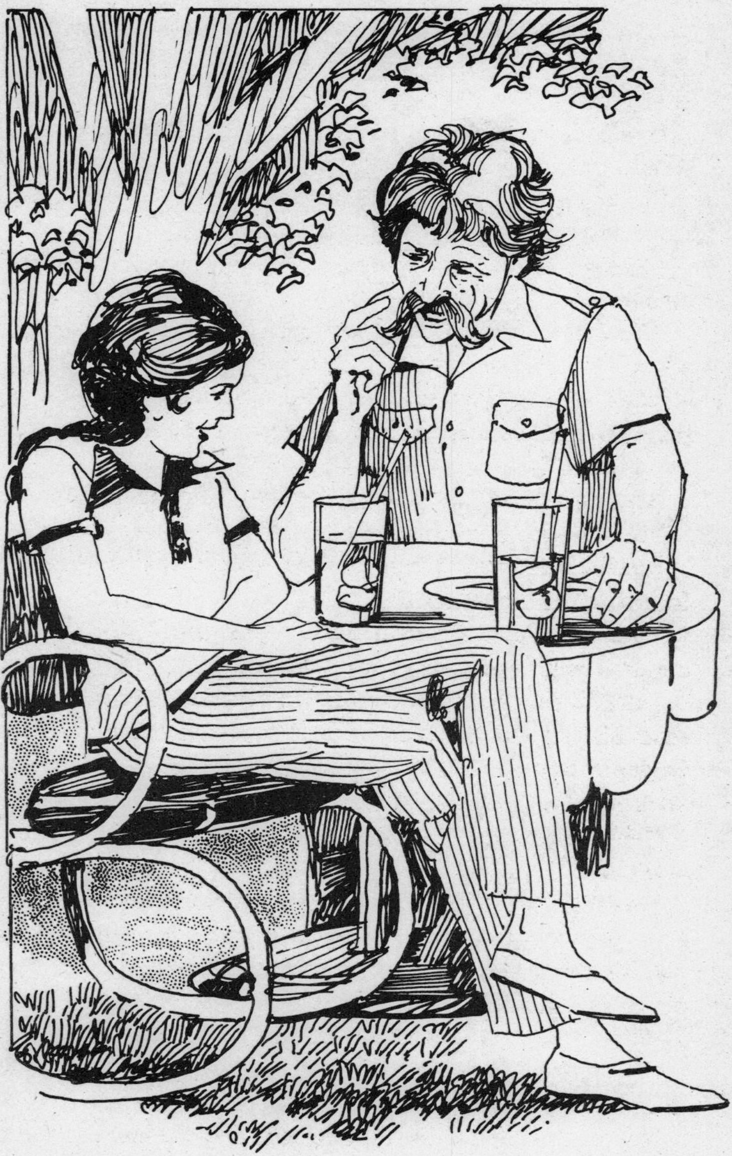

not liking it much. Uncle Gordon's words burned into her brain, and hurt her. She was consumed with anger and self-hatred. She had allowed everybody to push her around, from Uncle Gordon on down.

"Suppose I tried to escape," she said. "Would you let your dogs tear me apart? Or let me electrocute myself on your wall?"

Uncle Gordon surveyed her. "Yes, I would. I can't watch out for you especially. You're in danger, just like the rest of them. You have to move cautiously. Or boldly, if necessary."

"And die."

"Or win. Sometimes it comes down to that, Alison. And even if you win, there's no guarantee your reward will be gold and a prince. I found love easily, without fighting for it. And I lost it, before I really knew what I had. You have to make your moves and take the consequences. Or you can sit and snivel and curse your wasted life."

She was unreasonably angry. "You make it sound romantic and brave. But you spent your life amassing a dishonest fortune, and hurting others, destroying others, to keep it."

She turned back to the forest and the waning sun, her mind ablaze.

14 • Part of the Truth

Alison stirred, in a troubled sleep. Ugly dreams clawed at her, drew her back as she struggled to waken. A loud thudding seeped through her brain and she came awake suddenly, aware that the sound was a knocking at her bedroom door.

She sat up in bed, still dizzy with sleep. "Who is it?" she asked thickly.

"Ed Ginger. Foxworth wants everybody together for breakfast."

Alison sat on the edge of the bed. Something was obviously up. She washed and dressed quickly, choosing dungarees and a blouse. A small tremor of excitement passed through her; partly fear, partly anticipation. She looked out the window. The day was hazy and still.

She hurried downstairs, weaved her way through the hallways to the dining room. Faces turned to look at her, and she hoped her expression was not too foolish. Martin was there, flanked by Jill and Ted. She looked away from them. Jeff was there also, and he avoided her eyes.

Andrew and Laura Fallon were seated at the table, busying

themselves with halves of grapefruit. There were empty chairs for the others. Alison chose a seat across from the Fallons, down the table from Jeff, and from Martin and his friends.

A half grapefruit was before her, and she sprinkled sugar on it and began to eat. She usually liked grapefruit, but she found it hard to swallow now. Her stomach knotted.

A stirring at the doorway made her turn in her seat. Dana Mallory, Dr. Preston, and Cory Shaw entered in a single file, and quietly took seats. Alison sensed the repressed violence of their presence. One by one, they caught her eyes, bored into her: Dr. Preston, gross and perspiring; Cory Shaw, thin-lipped and nervous; and Dana Mallory, face unrelenting. Mistrusting each other, waiting for Alison to save them. For the high school student to bail out the super businessmen.

She couldn't eat. She lay down her spoon and one of the white-jacketed boys materialized to remove the offending grapefruit. Nobody spoke at the table. They resented being herded together like this, resented waiting for Uncle Gordon to arrive like a *deus ex machina.* But they all wanted out of this picturesque prison, so they summoned another ounce of patience.

Uncle Gordon appeared briskly, without fanfare, dressed in a crisp shirt and trousers. He took his seat at the head of the table. Incredibly, he dove into his grapefruit, eating it with calm enjoyment. The tension crackled.

When he'd finished, Uncle Gordon waved over a serving boy and the grapefruit rind was borne away. Uncle Gordon smiled at the group.

"We have sausage and eggs this morning," he said. "Cereal if you prefer."

Dr. Preston drummed anxiously on the table. Cory Shaw glared. "Don't push us," Shaw said.

Uncle Gordon put on a hurt expression. "Cory, it's only

Friday. You may get out of here early. Surely you should be grateful for that."

"Nobody's grateful," Dr. Preston said, looking straight ahead. "This has been a farce, and an insult."

"For the innocent," Uncle Gordon conceded. "But it's about to be over. I've observed you all for these few days, carefully considered the events of the week. I now know who shot at me, and tomorrow I'll take appropriate action."

Alison's heart pounded. Dr. Preston seemed to fill with fury. "*Tomorrow?*"

"Yes," Uncle Gordon said. "I though' I'd give you all a day to think about it. If the guilty party comes to me privately, everything can be accomplished quietly. I think that would be desirable."

"You're a sick man," Dr. Preston said.

Uncle Gordon's expression became solemn. "No, I'm not at all sick. I've indulged myself this week, I'll admit that. It's one of the pleasures of being wealthy. I've had you all squirming. But there is nothing sick about it. My purpose is practical. I'm saving my life. Now enjoy your breakfast."

The serving boy had brought out the platters of food and Alison forced herself to eat, as the others were doing. She was surprised to experience melancholy, almost regret that the adventure was ending. That made no sense, of course. All week she'd yearned only for escape.

Alison finished quickly and left the dining room. She wandered outside and strolled around the mansion, glancing balefully at the sky, which was filling with ominous clouds. The air was utterly still, the heat oppressive. She wondered who was guilty, and how Uncle Gordon knew. She also felt guilty herself. She'd flubbed her opportunity to solve the mystery. She almost believed now that Uncle Gordon had expected her to do this. He was obviously bailing her out at this point, before she got herself killed.

Still, she thought defiantly, it was his own fault. She'd never claimed to be able to outsmart people like this.

She realized suddenly that she was being followed, that she'd *been* followed since she left the house. She spun, and caught a glimpse of brown uniform disappearing around the corner. She ran after the escaping figure.

"William . . ." Her voice was hesitant, but he heard. He stopped, turned to stare at her, his body straining to run again.

She went to him, a little afraid. He glanced around, his eyes filled with terror. It was not the smug, slightly vicious William who'd driven her to Foxworth Hall.

She stopped when she reached him, and caught her breath. "Why do you follow me all the time?" she asked.

William ran a pink tongue across his thin lips. He looked more boyish than she'd remembered. "Don't tell him about Murdoch," William pleaded.

She brushed away a stray hair. "I won't. He'll find out anyway, sooner or later."

William looked sullen. "I needed the money. I have expenses."

"Is that why you stalked me in the woods?" she asked. "To ask me not to say anything?"

He looked at her with a mixture of malice and devotion that confused her. She was afraid of him. He finally shook his head no.

"Then why?" she asked.

He wore his shirt collar open, but otherwise he must have been sweltering in his uniform. His hair was damp and plastered over his pale forehead. "I kind of went for you," he said.

"Went for me . . ."

He was acutely embarrassed. "Yeah. I wanted to see you. But I knew you didn't like me, so I never talked to you."

She honestly didn't know how to handle it. "William, I'm sorry. You should have said something."

His eyes widened. "You would have gone with me?"

She tried to sound gentle. "No. I . . . well, probably not. But it's better than chasing me all the time."

William let out a short breath. He was jumpy, ready to run off like a flushed rabbit. "Listen, I got to go," he said. "The boss don't want me talking to guests."

"All right," she said.

He started, stopped, troubled by something. "I'd better tell you," he said.

"Tell me what?"

"I was going to ask you to go out with me . . . and tell you if you said yes. But you ought to know, anyway. I don't want you to get hurt."

She said, "Tell me what, William?"

He was in an agony of indecision. "You know that story he told?"

"Who?"

"The boss. That story, about someone taking a shot at him?"

"You heard about that?"

He nodded. "It made the rounds. But it's a lie. He never got shot at. Not with me, anyway. And that's what he said—that I was driving him that week in Westwood when he got shot at. But it never happened."

His voice became more defiant as he spoke. He was beginning to enjoy his perfidy. Alison nodded. "Thanks for telling me."

William half-shrugged. "I don't know what he's into this week. I don't understand what's going on. But with all the shooting and the dogs loose—I mean, this is a weird place. I don't want you to get hurt."

"Thank you."

He moved away from her, still unsatisfied, needing to say more. "Listen," he said, finally. "I had to drop out of school. My mother is sick. Otherwise, I would have went to college."

He reddened, then turned and ran. She watched him, shaken by his words. Cats looking at kings. The way she looked at Uncle Gordon, William looked at her. Proud and unattainable. It was educational. She had misread so many people this week. And she had been attractive to three men. Her eyes had certainly been opened.

She headed back to the house. The sky lowered now, threatening heavy rain. She needed to think. She wouldn't run to Jeff right away. She possessed the key—ironically enough, for the first time. She *knew* that Uncle Gordon had lied. But she didn't know why. Or what his intentions were. Or what he expected to happen.

She needed a cup of coffee now. And a stuffed chair in the foyer, and some time. The first two were simple enough. The last was a dwindling commodity.

Tension grew and spread like a virus and Alison began to feel a creeping insanity in the air as the afternoon passed. Lunch was a dismal affair. The chef had prepared an eye-catching salmon salad but nobody ate, except for Dana Mallory, who gorged himself conspicuously. Alison found it impossible to stay in the house trading nervous glances with the Fallons, Dr. Preston, and Cory Shaw as they all drifted from room to room. Dense clouds still loomed outside but there was dark blue sky beyond and it hadn't rained yet. She would risk being caught in a downpour.

She found herself headed for the forest again. The woods always seemed to call when she bowed under the weight of tension. She passed the sleeping dogs and plunged deep into the forest, keenly aware of the rustle of leaves, the chattering of birds and animals, and the earth odors. She was alone, the way Uncle Gordon must have been alone so many times over the years.

She ached, as he must have ached also, for things lost and never found. Alison was always known as the bright, enthusiastic, unflappable Thorne twin, the kid who ran from her darkroom to her music to who knows what else. Poor handsome Eric was subject to moods and dark humors, and how everyone petted him at those times. But Alison was always perky, always up. The woods knew better.

In her self-pity, she failed to hear the soft footsteps behind her. She gasped when a hand touched her back. But somehow, the hand was familiar, and she turned slowly. It was Martin.

"How did you get past the dogs?" she asked.

"Foxworth trained them to recognize me. That's how *you* get into the woods, isn't it?"

"Yes," she smiled. "He gave us the same path."

Martin smiled also, a strained smile. "Well, I guess he knew we'd have things to discuss. But I didn't come for small talk. I came to tell you a little truth."

There was a cold, ominous feeling about this meeting in the woods. Surrounded by the dark, damp greenery, the hoots and chitterings of animals, she felt conspiratorial, as if *she* were the unknown villain.

"What truth?" she asked.

"Foxworth seems to be ready to end this charade," he said. "I don't know what's going to happen when the fur flies. But you ought to be aware of how things stand."

Rain splashed them, a light drizzle. "Go ahead."

He caught her eyes with his very sincere gaze. It had convinced her on other occasions. "Alison, your great-uncle is a louse."

She laughed. "I know that, Martin."

"Well, he's more of a louse than you thought. He's about

to sell half of the east end of Long Island—and other choice parcels—to a foreign cartel."

Suddenly, she felt in control, almost excited. "Including some Arabs," she said. "And Mallory, Preston, and Shaw are in on it, and Andrew Fallon was supposed to grease the political wheels."

Martin looked stunned, and had a good deal of trouble recovering. She'd obviously spoiled a dramatic effect. "You knew?"

"Pretty much. I found evidence that the Arab delegation was here, at least. And I learned other things from other people."

"I see." He stumbled on his words now. "Well, I found this out some time ago, thanks to the investigation of Ted and Jill. Apparently, there's going to be a huge development corporation. Luxury condominiums out here in the estate country of the island, shopping malls in other parts of the east coast. Hundreds of thousands of spectacular acres will be shut in with gates, like the gates here, set aside for the wealthy and privileged. The return on the investment will be phenomenal, and the foreign cartel will get a foothold on U.S. land, just as it's getting a foothold in U.S. industry by purchasing plants and factories."

"And it's all being done quietly."

Martin studied her, trying to determine how much she knew. "I could win the election with this, and pretty much destroy your great-uncle. And your grandfather's credibility."

She nodded. "Yes."

He pursed his lips. "But I haven't. Not yet. I went to Foxworth first. I told him what I knew. I gave him a chance to avoid disaster, because I liked you, and I like your grandfather as a politician and as a man. I told Foxworth that I'd make it look as if he'd been approached and refused and was taking steps to halt the deal. He could have been a kind of hero."

She looked coldly at him. She wasn't angry at Uncle Gordon; she was angry at Martin. There was no reason for it; still, it was there.

"What did he say?" she asked.

"He said he'd think about it. And call me here when he'd decided. That's why I came so readily. But this is what he had in mind for an answer."

"I don't understand."

Martin laughed bitterly. "Alison, this is all a cover-up. I told you that from the beginning. I suspected at the start of the week what he was up to. I know it now. The potshot at me in the woods. The dogs getting loose. The cover story about an attack on him. Alison, he's going to have me killed."

It was plausible. And now that she *knew* Uncle Gordon had lied, it was imminent. "I can't believe that," she said.

"Believe it. Somehow, there'll be a melee. I'll be an unfortunate victim. I don't think he really meant me to die in the woods. That was a red herring. Now everyone thinks there's a nut loose with a gun. It's really very clever. I'm going to try to survive. If I don't, I thought somebody should know why I died."

So many pieces falling into place, and making no picture at all. Martin had made a beautiful case for his theory. So had Andrew Fallon. Paranoia ran rampant. And who was the assassin? Dana Mallory, who wanted to know the answers badly enough to terrorize Alison? None of it made sense. And the more truth she learned, the less sense it made.

"I don't know what to say," she told him. "I'm not used to games like this, where people get killed."

"Neither am I, Alison. Anyway, I'm getting back to the house. I won't make it easy for him. If we do survive this, remember to vote for me."

He grasped her hand briefly, firmly, let it go, and turned. She watched him walk briskly away from her and disappear around a curve. She didn't believe him. That was the awful part. She wondered what his motive was, as she wondered about Dana Mallory, and Dr. Preston, and Cory Shaw. Everybody was out for something at Foxworth Hall. And Uncle Gordon controlled it.

She began to walk again, toward the hunter's cabin. The drizzle stopped, leaving a wet mist in the forest. She tried to think logically, dispassionately. Uncle Gordon had called the shots from the word go. He'd chosen her path in the woods, made sure she knew about the hunters' cabin. With the *igal* behind the sofa. Behind there how long? Since Uncle Gordon put it there?

And Martin, assigned the same path. So they'd meet. Yes, Uncle Gordon knew his game. Now he was ready to end it. And she didn't know how.

She heard someone coming the other way and stopped, alert. She waited, listened to the droplets falling from leaves. Her throat tightened, and the air was too heavy to breathe.

Jeff came around a bend and her pulse resumed. She stood her ground until he was quite close to her. She realized that this was *his* path, too. How devilish of Uncle Gordon to encourage a romantic liaison.

"Hi," he said.

"Hi."

"I went to the cabin again. Looking for more clues. Nothing."

"Don't bother," she said. "You were right. There was a big meeting, and there is a foreign cartel and a land deal."

"How did you find out?"

"Martin Young followed me into the woods to tell me. He knew about the deal. He approached Uncle Gordon, to give him a chance to avoid a scandal. He thinks Uncle Gordon has arranged this whole charade to kill him."

Jeff looked honestly scared. "That's insane."

"Yes. So what?"

He made a wry face. "I don't know."

"I have more news," she said. "Uncle Gordon lied. William, the chauffeur, told me that nobody shot at Uncle Gordon."

Jeff's face was almost comic in its consternation. "Don't tell me *he* was infatuated with you."

"Yes," she said softly. She was so close to the edge of breakdown that it made no difference. "Why do you doubt me? Why do you doubt anything that happens here?"

"I don't," he said. "Not any more."

"There's something else."

"What?"

"I like you. I like you, and I don't want to fight over nonsense. I apologize for being foolish."

"What happened that day?" he asked.

"I was an idiot."

The woods sighed with the weight of rain in it, and there seemed to be a pulse in the air.

"I'm sorry, too," he said.

"No more apologies."

"Let's quit snooping," he said. "Let's keep low until this is over and then we'll get out of here."

She nodded, though she didn't agree.

"Think the house will be safe enough?"

"I doubt it."

"Maybe we can hide behind a tree."

She laughed.

A branch snapped, and she turned, drawing a breath. She knew who it was, knew they were watching her, from the moment Martin found her.

"What is it?" Jeff demanded.

"Nothing," she said.

He bit his lip and tried to look brave.

The clouds that gave no rain seemed to encourage a kind of hysteria in the afternoon. The guests gathered in the foyer, sitting stiffly, not talking, not daring to exchange glances. Alison sat with Jeff, and waited, and they all waited. The day darkened and nothing happened.

"I wish you had the rifle again," Alison said.

Jeff studied his hands. "Can't. Since that incident, and since Laura Fallon took one of the rifles, the gun rack has been emptied. Foxworth controls the distribution of firearms now."

"Well, that makes me feel safe."

Martin stood by the front window, peering out with a preoccupied look. He was remote from her, a lifetime apart. Still, the doubts lingered, the self-destructive questions about her ability to make wise decisions about people, to do the right thing.

"Maybe we should all go upstairs and to sleep," Jeff said. "It would pass the night."

"Nobody's going to sleep tonight," she said.

He nodded grimly. Dr. Preston stood up quite suddenly, causing a flurry of attention. His bulk commanded the foyer, and the abrupt fear on his face hushed what little conversation there was.

"Where's Dana Mallory?" Dr. Preston asked. "He's the only one missing. Does anybody know where he is?"

"I hope so," Ed Ginger said, entering the foyer. "He took a gun with him."

15 • The Whole Truth

People were on their feet. Alison looked quickly at Jeff, then at Ed Ginger. "How did he get a gun?" Cory Shaw demanded.

Ed looked embarrassed. His jaw was still swollen. "It was his own. We never confiscated it. But it's not in his room and neither is he."

Fallon seemed ready to faint. He shrank into his chair. "This is it," he muttered.

Martin turned from the window. "Are we going to look for him?"

The men blanched. "We ought to," Ed agreed.

"Why?" Dr. Preston said. "If we're all here together he can't do anything. Obviously, *he* took the shot at Foxworth. Let's get Foxworth into the room and stay here. What's Mallory going to do out in the woods?"

Foxworth had been standing in a doorway for a while, but he'd remained still. He coughed now and Dr. Preston looked at him. Foxworth came into the room.

"I don't think Mallory will do anything in the woods," he

said. "He knows he can't escape. I think he wants everyone to come looking for him. That will leave me vulnerable. Either I'd be out there, a sitting duck, or, more likely, I'd stay here, where he can get at me."

"There!" Dr. Preston said triumphantly. "So we stay here—all of us."

"No," Foxworth said. "If we don't force his hand, Mallory will get away with his attempted murder. And he'll try again, another time, when I'm not so well protected. I knew it was Mallory. I want a showdown."

"Which means what?" Martin asked.

"Which means that you will go out and look for him. And let him come back here."

"And kill you?" Ed Ginger said.

"I hope not," Foxworth replied. "The women will go to their rooms—after we search those rooms to make sure Mallory isn't already there. I have a gun of my own. I'll stay here in the foyer, with all the entrances in my sight."

"He'll shoot you through a window," Ed insisted.

"I'll be out of range," Foxworth said. "I know this house well. I know the angles, the mathematics of it. I'll be positioned quite safely."

"I don't like it," Ed grumbled.

"I'm not fond of it myself," Foxworth said. "But everybody went through some bad times this week for this moment. Let's not waste it now that it's here. Once we get this overwith, I'll extend my apologies to all, and you may leave in the morning."

"I'll buy that," Cory Shaw enthused.

"All right," Foxworth said. "Let's get started. Martin, go up and tell your cohorts about this. Let the girl stay in her room, of course. Ed will issue weapons."

Andrew Fallon turned white and stared at Laura. Alison bit her lip. She wondered if Uncle Gordon knew of Fallon's fears, or of Martin's. He must have known. If nobody shot at him, then Mallory's disappearance had to be a hoax.

Jeff grabbed her hand and breathed deeply. "Well," he said. "I get to be brave."

"I'm not brave," she said. "I'm really scared."

"Yeah. Well, if everything you say is true, the old man has something up his sleeve. I have to trust in that."

"Be careful," she said.

Under Ed Ginger's management, the search party was organized quickly. First, he led a careful search of the mansion, taking the individual bedrooms on his own, after arming himself. Satisfied that Mallory was not in the house, he took the men into the den where he brought out the hidden guns. Dr. Preston and Cory Shaw checked their weapons with cool expertise, and Alison watched them emerge into the foyer, remembering the interrogation she had suffered at their hands. Now they were obviously prepared to shoot their own partner. Alison reflected that she was becoming more inured to these evil people. Maybe that was a sign of maturity—or of cynicism.

Andrew Fallon held his rifle as if it were a cobra. He perspired freely, and Alison admired him. He was a foolish man, going out, so far as he knew, to meet his death. Yet he would not tell the truth and try to save himself. Ever the politician, he was more deeply afraid of scandal.

Martin held his gun almost jauntily, and Alison decided that he did not appear to be a man in fear of his life. He went upstairs, and Alison thought briefly that she would be alone here with Jill. She thrust the thought aside.

Jeff came to her, gripping his rifle tightly. He placed a hand on her arm.

"Lock your door and stay put," he said. "This may be a game, but a lot of nasty people are playing it. And I saw Ginger put real ammunition into these weapons."

She nodded. "I'd rather go with you."

Jeff smiled. "Your great-uncle chooses to be a chauvinist. Personally, I think you'd do as well with this gun as I will. You *did* capture Laura Fallon single-handedly."

"Shut up," she smiled.

Ed Ginger and Uncle Gordon completed the party. Martin came downstairs with Ted. As the others milled around, Ed Ginger took Ted into the den, and both emerged moments later, Ted carrying his rifle easily. He glanced at Alison, his face saying nothing.

"Okay," Uncle Gordon said. "Ladies upstairs."

Alison grasped Jeff's shoulder and wished him luck. She followed Laura Fallon up the stairs, Ed Ginger herding them. Laura went quietly to her room and Alison stepped into hers, closing the door behind her. She heard Ed locking the door from the outside.

"Don't try to come out," Ed told her. "No matter what you hear."

Alison sighed nervously, and paced. She went to the window, saw the men leaving the house and saw Ed direct them to split up. They trotted off into the darkness, which was now total and moonless under the nasty clouds. There was nothing but silence. She imagined Uncle Gordon, ensconced in a chair, gun across his lap, waiting. . . . For what? He knew he'd lied. He knew Mallory wasn't out for him. But then, where was Mallory?

She sat on the edge of her bed, trying to think of something to do. But her head was to full of thoughts. Uncle Gordon had lied. Martin had approached him with his knowledge of the big land deal. Fallon had approached him with his knowledge of the sabotage deal.

There was a link, a tenuous one. Uncle Gordon had found out a lot of things in a hurry. He'd learned that his secret land deal was no longer secret, that Andrew Fallon was not going to finagle legislation to enable the deal to go through, that Mallory, Preston, and Shaw had offered to destroy Martin Young in return for Fallon's favors. Certainly Uncle Gordon knew how desperate Mallory, Shaw, and Preston were to get money to solve their own personal problems. Desperate enough to do anything to make sure the land deal went through. Uncle Gordon knew that Young and Fallon were about to blow the whistle, that Uncle Gordon could therefore be in huge trouble with his foreign business partners who wanted to remain anonymous, that the reputation of E. Bradford Thorne could be badly tarnished because Gramps supported Fallon so openly.

Since Uncle Gordon controlled the deal, all of this knowledge put him in a difficult position. What *would* Uncle Gordon do about revelations like this?

Perhaps call everyone together for a week and get them nervous. If he was a man to be outraged by it all. Which still left a question: what was Alison Thorne doing here?

Assigned the same path as Martin Young and Jeff Harmon?

There was an answer hidden somewhere, but she wasn't seeing it. And no amount of tortured thought would solve it. Life was not a mystery movie. The pieces did not fall together neatly. Maybe they never did, for anybody.

She sat up suddenly, not breathing. She could have sworn she heard a noise . . .

A hand clamped over her mouth, cutting off her scream, and she was pulled backwards onto the bed. She saw Mallory now, caked with dirt. He stared at her wildly as he pinned her down.

"I'm going to take my hand away," he said, his voice strangely weak. "But if you scream, I'll kill you. I swear it."

He lifted his hand and she sucked in air, her heart thudding. Now she saw the dark hole in his shirt, near his left shoulder, and she saw the blood.

"How did you get in here?" she whispered. "They searched the rooms."

"I climbed up the outside wall," he said, breathing hard. "I hung from a cornice until they finished your room. Then I came in and hid in the closet. Marine training. Not easy to do with a slug in your arm."

Her mouth was dry. "Who shot you?"

"Never saw him. But he was good. I was walking in the woods. Thinking. Trying to dope things out. I heard someone following me. I took off, left the path. He stayed with me. He got off one shot before I lost him."

"Nobody heard a shot—"

Mallory smiled painfully. "He had my gun. With the silencer. He robbed my room."

She struggled to find a comfortable position, but he wouldn't allow her any movement. "They thought *you* took your gun and went out," she said.

"I know what they thought. I listened downstairs. When I heard their plan, I got the idea of climbing up here. Foxworth is wrong. I never shot at him."

"I know," Alison said, her body laced with agony. "Please let me up. I can't go anywhere."

He studied her for a long moment, then released her. She sat up, shuddering with relief. He stood, scrounged in his pockets for a small, thin cigar, and lit it. He was in obvious pain.

"You said you knew," he snapped. "What does that mean?"

She tried to still her racing pulse. "I knew that you didn't shoot at Uncle Gordon. Nobody did. His chauffeur told me."

Mallory half stumbled, pulled over a chair from the game table. He sat. "Nobody . . . I don't get it, then. Who took after me?"

"Who shot at Martin? Nobody knows . . ."

Her words stopped in her mouth and she looked at Mallory, not certain of her sanity. "What is it?" he demanded.

"I don't know. I had a thought. I was told—I don't know if it's true, though. I was told that Martin ordered Murdoch to loose the dogs."

Mallory chewed at the cigar. "What are you talking about?"

"The dogs," she said impatiently. "When Jeff was in the woods and the dogs were let loose. Martin was there too, and he shot them. But *Martin* ordered them loosed. He told Murdoch that Uncle Gordon had passed on the word. And Martin happened to be there, in time to save Jeff. But why would he want to put Jeff in danger, then save him?"

Mallory winced in pain. "Who cares?"

Alison rubbed her hands together, and they were clammy. "Unless Jeff wasn't supposed to be there. Is that possible? That Martin wanted to be in the woods *alone* when the dogs got loose? He had a gun. He would have saved himself. And it would have looked like somebody was out to kill him."

"I'm out to save my hide!" Mallory said.

Alison looked at him. "But maybe it's the same thing. Somebody shot at Martin in the woods. Maybe it was another hoax. Martin . . . well, Martin wanted me to think that Uncle Gordon was out to kill him."

Mallory's brows knit. "What?"

"It's complicated," she said. "It was a phony deal—like your deal, the one you tried to sell Andrew Fallon."

Mallory stormed to his feet shaky. "I'll kill him . . ."

"Yes," Alison whispered. "That's what *he* thinks, too. He thinks you're going to kill him, for telling Uncle Gordon. He thinks you and Uncle Gordon are in this together."

Mallory sat again, his eyes on Alison. Unless he was a superb actor, he was shocked. "Fallon went to Foxworth?"

Alison nodded. "Yes. He wanted no part of it."

Mallory laughed, a short, nasty laugh. "He was honest. So that's it. No wonder I couldn't get it. It's so impossible."

"What is?"

"That's why Foxworth got us here. Me, and Preston, and Shaw, and Fallon. He got sore that we tried the sabotage angle. He wanted to teach us a lesson. That's like him. Dramatic. So he scared the daylights out of us for a week. And Fallon sweated because he thought *we* were after *him*. It's beautiful."

It made good sense. "But it's not everything," Alison said. "Who shot at you? And why?"

Mallory held the cigar. "I don't know. But I can tell you one thing. The man is a pro. Only a sniper could track me like that, because I'm tops in the woods. This clown knew his way around. So you find me a veteran of jungle training, and I'll find my man."

Alison held her hands to her face, to control her shaking. She'd never been this frightened of anything. "What about a Vietnam veteran? Who saw a lot of action? A green beret?"

Mallory's eyes glittered. "He'd be the one."

"Yes, he would. And he'd be good enough to shoot Martin in the woods and not hurt him badly, making it look like a botched murder attempt."

"Who is it?" Mallory hissed.

The first crash at the door brought Alison to her feet. The second made her scream. The door flew open and Ted covered both her and Mallory with Mallory's rifle. His face showed no emotion.

"Keep quiet," he said.

"Why?" Alison asked.

"Because it has to be done. Jill told you that. And Mallory will be our scapegoat."

"What are you talking about?"

"Look out the window," Ted said.

Alison hurried to the window, looked down at the grounds outside the mansion, illuminated by the lights on the porch. Two figures left the house. One was Uncle Gordon, his hands clasped on top of his head. The other, holding a pistol at his back, was Jill.

Alison turned back to Ted. "You're going to kill him."

"Yes," Ted said simply. "He has to die. There's no other way to stop him. But we can't be implicated. So we need a killer. This week, this stupid scheme of Foxworth's, gave us the answer. Mallory. He tried to hurt you several times. He's the likely man to have shot at Foxworth before."

"Nobody shot at him," Alison said.

"We know. But nobody else does. Except for you, and the chauffeur. Both will be dead before morning. As well as Mallory, who got away the first time."

Mallory said nothing, but only watched with flickering eyes. Alison's stomach heaved; she thought she'd be ill. Ted sat down in a chair and held the rifle steadily, making escape impossible. Alison tried to think, but it was useless.

When Mallory moved, he surprised Alison. He dove, sliding across the floor, his hands reaching for the legs of Ted's chair. Ted had no opportunity to aim or shoot. Mallory yanked the chair toward him and Ted toppled over backwards, the gun falling from his hands.

"*Move!*" Mallory shouted.

Alison hesitated only an instant, then forced her legs to function. She ran from the room, down the hallway, and took the stairs two at a time. She wrenched open the front door and stumbled out into the hot night.

Jill was forcing Uncle Gordon down the path into the woods—down Alison's path. Alison ran silently, holding her breath until she was out of range of the lights, and swallowed up in darkness. She'd have to find a rock and throw it at Jill. There was no way to fight her, not when she carried the gun.

She neared the path, slowed her pace to avoid being heard. She threw back her head to find air, clenched her teeth at the stinging bites of insects. She didn't dare slap at them.

There were sizable rocks at the side of the path. One of them would do the job, if she aimed straight. She had no choice. She wouldn't allow herself to think about it.

She stepped onto the path, and the dogs leaped to their feet, lunging at her. She screamed and fell back. Jill grasped Uncle Gordon's collar and forced him to turn.

Jill smiled. "I knew I might be followed. So we switched the dogs around. Ted is very good with dogs. He worked with killer dogs in the service. Nobody can use these paths now, except for me. Because none of them will attack Foxworth, and I'm right behind him."

The dogs snarled at Alison. "What happened, Uncle Gordon?"

Uncle Gordon grimaced. "I expected an attempt from Martin. But not such a serious one. I wasn't prepared for two assailants, from two directions."

Alison was numb now. "Why Martin?"

"He came to me," Uncle Gordon said. "He'd discovered a bit of skullduggery. There's no time now to explain . . ."

"I know about it," Alison said. "Martin told me he gave you a chance to be graceful about it. And this week was your answer. You intended to have him killed."

Uncle Gordon smiled, his face chiseled in the wooded darkness. "He twisted the facts slightly. You see, I already knew about the deal with Andy Fallon, before Martin came to me. Because by that time, I'd had my own people do some investigating. The land deal looked too good, too profitable, too easy. Suddenly, a mysterious foreign cartel approaches me, lays out a mouth-watering proposition. Encourages me to contact my business partners. Of course, the deal would require legislative chicanery, something Andy Fallon could manage—*if* he wanted to keep his Senate seat."

Alison felt icy cold. "What are you getting at?"

"Martin Young is really a brilliant young man. A very committed young man as well, a young man obsessed with getting into the Senate and destroying capitalists like me. So obsessed that he wanted to insure his election. So he took his cue from the FBI's ABSCAM investigation, and he created a phony foreign cartel. I pretended to bite. Then Martin had one of his people, posing as a cartel member, suggest to my partners that they offer Andy Fallon the sabotage proposal. It was all very neat. There would be a monstrous scandal, and Martin Young would bust it wide open, destroy Andy Fallon, become a hero, and get elected."

"That's enough!" Jill snapped. "I don't want to hear any more stories. Ted should have killed Mallory by now. Once he brings him here, we'll kill you and Alison. It will look like an attack by Mallory, repulsed by you, resulting in tragedy for all. And the world will be rid of Gordon Foxworth."

Alison shivered with cold, even in the warm night. Her death was minutes away, but there was an unreality to it. She still believed the others would find them. They wouldn't, of course. Alison prayed with silent intensity, hoping God would see fit to forgive Uncle Gordon's trespasses and prevent her death.

"Can't you call the dogs off?" Alison asked Uncle Gordon. "Or make them attack Jill?"

Uncle Gordon made a wry face. "The barrel of her pistol is against my spine. The words would never leave my lips."

"Exactly," Jill said.

Alison looked at Jill, slender and beautiful in the darkness. It was impossible. She had to turn and run. But Jill would shoot her. She had to try . . . desert Uncle Gordon, save herself. But she couldn't do that, and she was glad she couldn't.

She heard the noise to her left, but Jill didn't. Alison kept her mouth shut. She must not betray an emotion. She rubbed her moist palms against her jeans, waiting.

When it happened, it was over too quickly to see. Murdoch came out of the foliage, stumbling as he did so. Jill's head twisted, and her gun shifted. But Murdoch was already shouting at the dogs.

The animals obeyed their old master. They turned from Alison and hurled themselves at Jill, forcing her back until she screamed and crumpled under their weight.

Uncle Gordon called off the shepherds and they backed away, crouching and snapping. Jill lay curled on the dark earth, bloodied. She breathed raggedly, eyes shut, sobbing.

Uncle Gordon stooped and took up the pistol. He turned to Murdoch. "I thought I fired you."

Murdoch seemed small and humble. "Ye never could take care of yourself."

Uncle Gordon looked down at the ground. "No," he said huskily. "I never could. Let's go back to the house and hope that Mallory is still alive."

Mallory was sitting on Alison's bed, swaying, but hanging on to the rifle. He had Ted well guarded. Ted sat morosely in a chair, looking disgusted with himself.

"I would have helped you," Mallory said dimly. "But I don't think I would have made it downstairs."

Uncle Gordon took the rifle from him. "Lie back. The others should be here soon. And I believe there's a doctor in the house."

The others trickled back within the next half hour, and within an hour, Mallory was in his own bed, the bullet removed and the wound bandaged and dressed by Dr. Preston. An ambulance had been called. Now Dr. Preston sat in the foyer with the others. Jill and Ted were conspicuously absent. They'd been tied up in the den and were being guarded by Ed Ginger until the police arrived.

Allison sat next to Jeff. Martin stood, stunned and pale. He didn't need to be guarded; he wasn't going anywhere. Andrew Fallon looked chipper and delighted. His wife was not as happy. The terrors would never be over for her, as long as Fallon remained in politics.

"I realized what my life had become," Uncle Gordon said, addressing the guests. "And I knew that it was over—the seclusion, the burying of my head in Foxworth Hall. If I was nothing more than a source of income and influence for desperate men, then I'd wasted my years. I wanted to do something to atone, or at least to put a credit mark in my ledger.

"This was it. I wanted to save my great-niece from a tragic mistake that would publicly embarrass her and her grandfather, and I wanted to show my three colleagues what ugly men they'd become. Just this side of killing me for their own personal reasons, clinging to me for my name and the possibility that I would save them. It's a sad little picture. I think I achieved my purpose this week. Of course, I had not counted on Mr. Young and his friends being quite so vicious and obsessed. I underestimated them, and other people. I endangered Alison. I am truly sorry for that. I do hope Mr. Young is sorry as well."

Martin only stared, fairly well destroyed. Alison tried not to look at him.

"Martin," said Uncle Gordon, "you and your adjutants began to believe in your own pure righteousness. Nobody is that righteous. Only God, and He doesn't get involved in politics, no matter *which* party claims him during campaigns."

Uncle Gordon now looked at Alison.

"I'm very glad you met Mr. Harmon, Alison. I wasn't really trying to make a match, however. I wanted this honest and energetic young reporter present at these proceedings. He deserves a scoop to boost him on his way."

"It's a bigger one than I expected," Jeff said.

Uncle Gordon smiled, but a lot of tar had been taken out of him. "Yes. So friends, I've expiated one folly by rehiring Murdoch. As far as land deals, and my business colleagues in this room, I can't promise that I'll distribute my worldly goods among the poor and devote myself to good works. I like business, I like money, and I even like these reprehensible men. However, I *can* promise to be more careful—and even a bit more benevolent, perhaps. That may mean, Alison, that some of my fortune may be gone by the time I die."

"I don't want your fortune, Uncle Gordon," Alison said quietly. "I would like to get to know *you*—without this much excitement."

Uncle Gordon raised a hand. "I promise to invite you back, with your brother, for a peaceful weekend. Anyway, I think you've learned something about managing your life and dealing with other people, and that's a good legacy."

Alison nodded. "Yes, it is."

She looked around at the brooding faces of Dr. Preston and Cory Shaw. She thought of Mallory. Avoided Martin. Glanced at the Fallons. She'd remember them vividly.

And she'd remember Uncle Gordon, with guilty fondness. She smiled at him now as he gave her a secret look.

The reunion with Dad and Eric was emotional, with hugs and kisses and a babble of excited chatter. Eric was burned brown and bursting with questions. Dad was quietly concerned with Alison's haunted look. The flight back to Ivy was mostly small talk, but once home, Alison told the entire story, in a soft voice shuddering at some of the memories. Dad and Eric listened intently, Eric clenching his fists tightly at some points.

Gramps arrived later that week, and Alison told the story again, her second "debriefing," as she jokingly called it. Gramps listened with bright, intense eyes, and often interrupted with questions. When she'd finished, Gramps hugged her gently and then said, "Are you okay?"

She nodded.

"Never will I expose you to that kind of danger again," he promised. "I was a fool. I won't forgive myself easily."

She dug her fingers affectionately into his shoulders. "No. Don't blame yourself. Uncle Gordon told you he suspected something about Martin Young, and that he wanted the chance to show me the truth. It sounded reasonable. Even Uncle Gordon didn't expect some of the things that happened."

"He should have," Gramps said bitterly. "He had no right to endanger your life that way. I don't care what lesson he wanted you to learn. I will see him, and I'll set him straight."

Alison had rarely seen Gramps so angry, and she decided not to defend Uncle Gordon further. Uncle Gordon was a strong man, and he could defend himself—and be big enough to admit he was wrong. She only regretted that she wouldn't be allowed to sit in on the confrontation between her grandfather and her great-uncle.

She smiled at Gramps, sheepishly. "Well, at least I *did* learn the truth about Martin Young."

Gramps nodded. "Which should not ever prevent you from supporting any candidate you believe in, whether I support him or not."

"I know," she said. "Andy Fallon didn't turn out to be such a pillar of strength and virtue either, though he turned out to be honest."

"Relatively honest," Gramps said sardonically. "I have to have a talk with Andy as well. He's had an honorable career and it may be time to take it in another, less exhausting direction. I may have an appointive post or two the President will agree to. And I think Laura will be happier as well."

Alison kissed him impulsively. "You're super, Gramps!"

"So are you," he smiled, as he blushed.

She exhaled and nodded. "Sometimes. And sometimes confused. I still don't know exactly what I'm going to do with my life, but I know it's going to involve working with people. I misread so many characters at Foxworth Hall, found out so much about what makes people tick inside. It's not just good guys and bad guys, and I want to find out more. Lots more."

Gramps glanced at Alison's father, who nodded. Dad said, "Making people your profession is always a good choice. They'll never bore you."

"That's for sure." She felt warm and protected between her father and her grandfather. She wanted to spend some time with Eric now, who'd left for a lunch date. And she wanted to ask Dad if she could invite Jeff Harmon to Ivy, or down to Washington, now that his big exposé in a Long Island newspaper had made him a big media star.

But all that could wait just a little while. First, she wanted to shower and change and go out into the sweltering summer streets of Washington, to walk and walk and walk anywhere she wanted. Without feeling trapped.

"It's good to be free," she said to Gramps and Dad, and she filled with the emotion of what she'd said. There were many kinds of freedom, and even rich and powerful men like Mallory and Preston and Shaw—and Uncle Gordon sometimes—found themselves imprisoned and mercilessly hunted on a dark forest path. Alison had found her way into the sunshine, and she decided to stay there for as long as she could.

Thorne Twins Adventure Books

by Dayle Courtney

#1—Flight to Terror Eric and Alison's airliner is shot down by terrorists over the African desert (2713).

#2—Escape From Eden Shipwrecked on the island of Molokai in Hawaii, Eric must escape from the Children of Eden, a colony formed by a religious cult (2712).

#3—The Knife With Eyes Alison searches for a priceless lost art form on the Isle of Skye in Scotland (2716).

#4—The Ivy Plot Eric and Alison infiltrate a Nazi organization in their hometown of Ivy, Illinois (2714).

#5—Operation Doomsday Lost while skiing in the Colorado Rockies, the twins uncover a plot against the U.S. nuclear defense system (2711).

#6—Omen of the Flying Light Staying at a ghost town in New Mexico, Eric and Alison discover a UFO and the forces that operate it (2715).

#7—Three-Ring Inferno The twins find jobs with the circus, and must rescue a friend from a motorcycle gang (2892).

#8—Mysterious Strangers Strange look-alikes lead Eric and Alison into a tangle with an international spy ring in Egypt (2893).

#9—The Foxworth Hunt Alison is imprisoned on her uncle's estate, and must find out which of his other guests wants to murder him (2894).

#10—Jaws of Terror Eric must search through shark-infested waters to solve the mystery of his friend's father's disappearance (2895).

#11—The Hidden Cave The twins travel to a tiny island kingdom in the Aegean Sea, where they become involved in a civil war (2896).

#12—Tower of Flames Eric and Alison are trapped inside a building taken over by terrorists (2897).

Available at your Christian bookstore or

STANDARD PUBLISHING